No Greater Love

# No Greater Love

**Edwina Orth**

iUniverse LLC
Bloomington

# No Greater Love

iUniverse books may be ordered through booksellers or by contacting:

iUniverse LLC
1663 Liberty Drive
Bloomington, IN 47403
www.iuniverse.com
1-800-Authors (1-800-288-4677)

ISBN: 978-1-4917-0615-2 (sc)
ISBN: 978-1-4917-0617-6 (hc)
ISBN: 978-1-4917-0616-9 (ebk)

Library of Congress Control Number: 2013916534

Printed in the United States of America

iUniverse rev. date: 09/13/2013

With thanks to my son, Frank, his lovely wife, Karen, and all my family. They have always been supportive with love and good advice. Thanks also to friends Dottie, Charlie, and Fred. Your help has been invaluable to me.

# Chapter One

Mathew walked along the path that led to the lake. He dew in deep breaths of the cool air. God, how good it felt to be outdoors at last. His eyes roved over the landscape, taking in the fall colors. So far, they were mostly gold or light brown. He flexed his shoulders as he felt the cool breeze. It was early September, and already Vermont had coolness in the early morning breeze. He wore an Irish fisherman's sweater over a flannel shirt. He liked an early morning walk. It cleared his mind and helped start the day right.

He thought of his computer repair job, and he began to review the work he had done yesterday. The work he had just completed had been more complicated than usual, and he had put in lots of overtime while finding the cause of the trouble. Computers could be tricky, but he really loved his job.

It was his coworker, Charlie, who bugged him. Mathew had to explain so many things to him that he wondered if Charlie knew anything about computers. Charlie had been working for the company for over a year. He had seniority, and he knew it. It took all of Mathew's patience to deal with Charlie's smug attitude. *Someday I'll have enough money saved so I can quit this job at B and B computers and have my own business.*

He rounded the bend and saw the lake ahead of him. Gulls wheeled over the water with their harsh cries, looking for food. He stood for a while absorbing it all—the mountains in the distance and the sun reflected on the water. He became conscious of someone watching him. It was a girl, perhaps twelve or thirteen years old, sitting with an open book cradled in her arms.

He waved and almost turned to leave when he heard her hiccup. Was she crying? He looked more closely and saw her red eyes and tear-stained face. Slowly he walked up to her. "Are you okay?" he asked. "Can I be of help?"

She shook her head and murmured, "No thanks."

Mathew felt her cool, wary stare and backed away. He decided that she was better off left alone. He might frighten her if he probed.

He turned and began walking back to his house, a small Cape Cod. It was made of wood and stone. He had lived in it for two months. He felt lucky to have found it before he had started his new job. There was still open country around, and Lake Champlain was special. The Adirondacks were across the lake. He never would be tired of looking at those rugged peaks.

He saw a woman running toward him. She was dressed in form-hugging jeans and a blue sweater.

Her auburn hair was awry, and her expression was anxious. "Have you seen a young girl anywhere up the path? I have to find her."

Mathew nodded. "Yes, there is a girl reading by the water. I guess she's about another hundred feet or so. She looked to be crying, but I am not sure."

"Thanks." If possible, the woman ran faster, and she soon was around the bend and out of sight.

*I wonder who they are and where they are from. I haven't seen then around before.* There were several homes nearby, but he hadn't met any neighbors yet. *I wonder if that is her daughter. If so, she's very young to have a child that age.*

Kathy waved good-bye to the man. Knowing that her daughter was close, she ran even faster and almost stumbled in her haste. Her daughters had just come back from a visit with their father. They were always upset and hard to deal with after seeing him. She had tried to figure it out and had come to the conclusion that he was still angry with her because of the divorce.

It was hard for them to understand. They wished that the family could be together again. Kathy never bad-mouthed their father, but she was aware that he made untrue remarks about her to the children.

When Kathy saw her daughter with red, puffy eyes, she stopped to gain some poise. *What can I do to help her? What makes her so hard to understand?* It had to be more than just a visit to her father. *Is she unhappy at school? She seems to have few friends, and she says that some of the girls lie about her. They say Lisa tells whoppers.* Mrs. Tyson, her teacher, had recommended a child psychiatrist. *She even gave me several names for me to call. I'm not ready for that yet. That just might upset Lisa and make her mistrust me even more.*

Kathy said, "Lisa, I've been looking all over for you. You've been crying. What's wrong? You know you only have to tell me, and I'll do all I can help you."

Lisa glared at her mother and turned her head away. Finally, she said, "You'll never understand. Daddy's not interested in me. The girls at school all hate me. You're so busy with your job that you don't have time to listen to me or even want to."

"I am sorry that you're upset. I do listen when I can, but you tell such stories that people just don't believe you anymore. If you told the truth, without adding all those imaginary tidbits, you would be believed. Also, you know that I have to work. We need the money that my job brings in, and that can't be changed."

"You wouldn't have to work if you and Dad were together again."

Kathy bit her tongue. Lisa didn't understand and probably never would. Kathy hadn't told her any of the reasons for the divorce. It would not be right to tell her of the abuse and unfaithful behavior. *How do you explain psychological abuse or a hateful, destroying relationship to a child?*

"Let's not go there, Lisa. I will not say any harsh words about your father. However, I had my reasons for what I did. Come on now. Lunch is waiting, and I promised to take you and Noreen to the mall this afternoon."

Lisa's face brightened, and she rose to follow her mother. Lisa was a slim, gangly girl. She had dark blue eyes and attractive auburn hair. She was never happy with her looks and seemed ill at ease. She was still growing and uncomfortable with it.

"Mom, there was a strange man who walked close to me as I was reading. He tried to talk to me, but I didn't answer him. He looked weird. Do you know him? I never saw him before. He had a scowl on his face, and I was afraid."

Kathy didn't reply for a moment. Then said, "I met him too. I asked if he had seen you. He seemed very nice to me. He said that he had noticed you reading. I don't think you should judge someone so quickly, but you were right to be cautious. He may live on our street. The house that was vacant for months is now occupied. He may be our new neighbor."

"Well, I don't like him. He was rude and scared me. I hope we don't ever see him again."

Kathy thought about what her daughter had said. The man had been pleasant and helpful. He didn't seem to be a person to be afraid of. Her daughter was getting more and more difficult to understand. Perhaps she was wrong to refuse the help of a child psychiatrist. However, that was a last resort.

## Chapter Two

After saying good-bye to the woman, Mathew left the walking path and turned onto his block. As he neared his house, he thought of how lonely his life was. He had moved there from Atlanta and had made no friends. The bar scene didn't appeal to him, and most of his coworkers were married. Perhaps he should get a dog. There was lots of room in his yard to keep a dog happy. He could put up a fence so the dog could be safe from traffic. He imagined a black or yellow lab. In his mind, he could almost hear a yap, yap as he came closer to his house.

He had heard right. Sure enough, a mangy dog was sitting close to his house. He couldn't tell the breed, and it looked like it had been dumped in grease and dirt. He didn't see a collar.

Mathew walked up to the shivering dog. "Now where did you come from?" As he looked into the pleading eyes of the sorry creature, he shook his head. "I think a bath first, then some food, and a place to sleep until I can find your owner."

He went into the house through the back door. He changed into old jeans and an even older shirt.

He went back outdoors to the shivering dog. He took a short rope, placed it around the dog's neck, and led it into the garage.

There was a utility room off the garage with a deep washtub for heavy-duty cleanup work. The dog wasn't happy and jerked wildly to be free.

When Mathew finally got the dog into the tub, he quickly began to shampoo and rinse off the shivering dog. He had to shampoo the dog three times before he was clean. When the job was finished, the garage needed cleaning too, but the dog looked and smelled much better.

Soon, the bowl of water was almost empty, and Mathew wondered what to feed the starving dog. He decided on scrambled eggs and some well-cooked bacon. After downing it in a hurry, the dog rolled over and held up his paws, almost asking for a good rub. Mathew patted the dog's head and belly and laughed at how easily the dog had gotten what he wanted. It seemed as if Mathew had found a friend at last. Mathew looked the dog over carefully and decided he was a mixed breed.

Later that evening, Mathew put the rope around the dog's neck and took him for a walk. The dog tired easily, and Mathew brought him back and found an old blanket for a sleeping pad. After circling several times, the dog gave a soft woof and settled in for the night.

Mathew was too wired to sleep. He thought of how strange the day had been. If he could not find

the dog's owner, he would like to keep him. After he
fell asleep, the furry body snuggled next to him.

Mathew groggily opened his eyes. The dog was
resting on his bed. He woofed softly and darned if
he didn't seem to smile. Mathew dressed in jeans
and a sweater; after securing the rope around the
dog, he took him for a long walk. The morning was
cloudy and cool, just right for September. The leaves
were turning, and there was a nip in the air. The dog
chased leaves and looked up to see if Mathew had
noticed his antics.

As he turned to go home, he saw a woman and
a dog walking toward him. As she drew closer, he
recognized her as the woman who had been looking
for her daughter. As they drew closer, he noted her
slim but rounded figure, her neat wavy auburn hair,
and her thoughtful look.

"Good morning," Mathew said with a smile.
"Do you recognize this dog? I found him sitting
by my house yesterday. I believe he may have been
abandoned or separated from his owner. By the way,
my name is Mathew Kennedy. My nickname is Skip.
I live in the last house on this road—the one with the
blue trim."

"Good morning, Mr. Kennedy. I live on this street
too, the third house down on the left. How did you
get that nickname?"

"When I was in college, I did some volunteer work
with some teenage boys. I taught them karate. I used
to skip a little before I gave the high kick that helped

them defend themselves. They called me Skip, and it just stuck, I guess."

"I would have liked to have seen you do that. My name is Katherine Hilliard, and Kathy is the short version. I haven't seen this dog before. He seems to like you though. Perhaps you can keep him."

"Yes, I'd like to. I first have to find out if he has an owner somewhere. I plan to visit several veterinarians. Perhaps they will recognize him."

"That's a great idea. You ought to get him checked out by one of them if you plan to keep him. They can give you lots of good information on feeding, training, and exercise. What are you going to call him?"

Mathew rubbed his face. He thought about a name, but nothing came to mind. "I guess I'll have to decide that later. He may already have an owner and a name."

A shrill voice yelled, "Mother! You're wanted on the phone. Hurry up!"

"I guess I'd better run on home. There may be a phone call. My daughter gets things mixed up at times." With a smile and a wave, Kathy hurried toward her house.

When Kathy came into the living room, there was no one on the phone.

"I guess they hung up," Lisa said.

Kathy sighed. "Why didn't you take down their name for me? You know how to answer the phone properly; you just don't take the time."

"Sorry, Mom. I'll do better next time."

When Lisa left the room, Kathy could swear she heard a giggle. A frown marred Kathy's face as she recalled several calls from Josh, a man she sometimes dated, that she had not been told about. *Is Lisa trying to interfere with my social life? If so, why?*

# Chapter Three

Mathew made several trips to local veterinarians. None had seen the dog before. He had the vet closest to his house give the dog a checkup. To be on the safe side, the dog got a rabies shot and flea protection.

"I guess you are going to be staying with me, fuzzy face. At least I hope so."

A tired woof made Mathew realize that the dog was just plain tuckered out. He pulled into his garage and decided to feed the dog and take him outdoors for a few minutes.

Later, after fixing his own dinner, Mathew did some work on his computer and watched television for a while. Before bed, he took the dog for another walk. He passed by Kathy's darkened house. He imagined her ready for bed, dressed in a sheer nightgown. He could not get her out of his mind as he walked home. *Did she have a special relationship with someone? Would she go out on a date with him?*

He laughed at his daydreams. He'd only just met her—and now he was planning strategies to get closer to her. She was already burdened with an ex-husband, two daughters, and if he guessed right, more than a few problems. Divorces were usually messy, and he felt her divorce was still causing the family stress. Still, he thought, she was really lovely, and he would like to have someone special in his life. Not just someone though, but an auburn-haired, warm bit of femininity.

He had to get her out of his mind if he ever wanted to get to sleep. He tried thinking of names for the dog. Finally he chose Skipper and drifted asleep, only to dream of an auburn-haired woman with sparkling eyes, a turned-up nose, and a cute, rounded derrière.

<hr />

Waking early, Mathew quickly dressed and took Skipper for a short walk. He decided that he couldn't leave the dog alone in the house all day. He needed to be fed, watered, and walked. He decided to take him to work until he could get a fence built. He remembered to take a bowl for water and some kibbles for Skipper's lunch.

Mathew called several contractors for a price quote on the fence. He chose a metal one with a gate that attached to the house. The dog should be safe there and be able to run and play. He thought of how his life had changed in just a few days. The stray dog had cost him money—and would cost even more with the fence—but he would have fun watching

Skipper chase his tail, run to greet him, and snuggle close at night. Yes, it was worth every penny.

He took Skipper to work with him every day that week. The dog seemed to know he was to keep quiet and stayed under the desk until Mathew could take him outside for his noon walk and lunch.

By Tuesday of the following week, the fence was up. He knew that Skipper would not like staying at home, but it was the best he could do for now. Each night, he took the dog for a long walk, and soon a routine was set. A lasting bond had been forged between man and dog.

---

Mathew was in the yard playing with Skipper when Kathy stopped at the fence with her dog. He felt a jolt of happy surprise as he looked at her soft hair and gentle smile. She wore jeans, a lavender sweater, and walking shoes with purple laces. She looked more like twenty than the thirty-six he thought she was.

"Hi, Kathy," he said and gave her a welcome wave. "Come on in and bring your pooch with you. I think they will get along okay. Skipper isn't a vicious dog— just a little afraid of anything new. He still has to get used to things here."

Kathy opened the gate and brought in her dog. "My dog's name is Sheeba. She is spayed, of course, and is six years old."

Mathew leaned down to pet the dog. Sheeba wiggled in ecstasy. Skipper came over to touch noses with his new friend, and as soon as Kathy undid the leash, they ran and jumped together. It looked as if they were playing tag. The dogs wore themselves out and collapsed in a heap.

The antics of the dogs lifted Kathy's spirits. She was laughing, and Mathew couldn't take his eyes off of her. "Want to come in for a cup of tea or coffee?" he asked.

"Okay. That would be nice."

Except for a few dates with Josh, Mathew was the first man she'd taken notice of since her divorce. Mathew was slim and muscular. His face made her look twice, and she noticed his strong chin, healthy complexion, and dark brown eyes. He had a unique quietness about him, a composed confidence that made her want to trust him.

He showed her his small garden. It was only a few rows of herbs, but he explained how it would get better the next year. He said with pride, "This is my first try at growing my own kitchen garden. I like to have fresh spices and herbs ready to use."

Kathy raised her eyebrow. "You mean to say you cook?"

"Well, I do some of it. Eating out gets expensive, and the only way I can have really fresh, tasty food is to cook it myself."

"Your momma raised you right!" Kathy said with a grin. "How about doing the dishes?"

"I do them too. Otherwise I'd turn into a bachelor slob."

Kathy smiled in approval.

Mathew had decorated the house with soft tans, some mauve, and bright turquoise. Each room looked inviting.

Kathy noticed the details in the chair rails and moldings. There were pictures of landscapes and sea scenes on the walls.

While they sat at the kitchen table and sipped tea and ate scones, the dogs began barking loudly. Mathew looked out into the yard and saw Kathy's daughter trying to get into the yard. He went to the backdoor and called, "Hello. If you want to come in, come to the front door."

She walked to the front of the house, and Mathew opened the door. He said, "Come in, Lisa. Your mother's here. Is there anything wrong? Can I be of help?"

"Nothing's wrong except that I have homework to do, and I need my mother to help me."

"What kind of homework? Maybe I can help. I used to be a tutor."

"No, thanks. My mother knows what I have to do for this science paper."

Kathy came into the hall and overheard them. She said, "Lisa, I will be home in a few minutes. I'd like to finish my tea first. You go along, and I will be there shortly."

Lisa wanted to explode. *She is getting too cozy with that man. I hate him. Hate him! When I see Dad, I'll tell him all about what's going on. Maybe I can go home again to live when he finds out she's going to Mathew's house. She's supposed to be taking care of me—not getting goofy over a man. I'll tell Dad. He'll know what to do.*

When Kathy arrived home, she found that the science project was not that difficult. Lisa did not need her help to finish it at all. She wondered if Lisa would ever begin to mature. She seemed to need a lot of emotional support. The visits to her father made things worse, at least they appeared to. Lisa had not been close to her father when they were all together, so why did she crave her father's approval now?

As much as she hated to, she felt that Lisa's father should be taken into her confidence. He had never been eager to talk about the girls before, but this was getting out of control. Surely he would want to help if he knew how much Lisa lied. It had been after the divorce that Lisa had begun to be sullen, withdrawn, and started lying. The lying had become a much bigger problem. She was alienating herself from her friends at school as well as those at church. Friends Lisa used to invite for an overnight were not mentioned now. Her confrontational attitude kept friends away.

*I want to help Lisa, but if the girls at school find out she was seeing a psychiatrist, they would make her life unbearable. I'll wait a few more months; if there is no change, I'll make an appointment with a good child psychiatrist.*

Lisa's father should be involved. Bruce didn't find Lisa's lying a problem, but he did not know how many lies she had told. The ones she made up about Mathew watching her were more than weird. Did her father have anything to do with this new phase? Kathy shook her head. No, she was sure he wasn't that mean.

---

Lisa worked on her science project for a while. She knew it was going to be okay. Science was her best subject, and she always got good grades. She wondered if the new friend of her mom's would have offered anything new. He spoke as if he really wanted to help her, but her dad had said that she should be wary of him.

Her dad didn't want her mother to get involved with anyone. He was pissed off because of the divorce. Lisa wished they could be a family again. Maybe her dad would pay attention to her if they all got back together.

*I do love Mom, but I wish Dad would love me too. I have always tried to please him, but when Mom and Dad got the divorce, I had to come live with Mom. I only get to see him on weekends. If Mathew and Mom marry, I will never see much of Dad. I'll do anything I can to stop that. Mathew will never be a father to me. I hate him. I'll make sure Dad knows about Mathew and Mom's visit to his house. He asked me to tell him if Mom did anything unusual.*

Lisa decided to tell her sister about finding their mom visiting their new neighbor. "Hey, Noreen, I've finished my science project. How about walking to the lake?"

Noreen sat at her desk and finished writing a few sentences. She looked up at her sister and smiled. She was ten years old and had a happy way of looking at things. Her short, wavy, dark hair framed her face. She had the same brown eyes as her mother did.

"Okay. I don't have much more homework to do. I can finish it later."

Lisa said, "I think this new guy is out to get close to Mom. If Mom gets to like him, there won't be any way we can all be a family again."

"Lisa, you just don't want to remember how Mom and Dad used to argue. Dad was not always good to Mom. That's why they got the divorce."

"I don't think Dad was ever mean to Mom. She often came home from work late, and she didn't tell Dad where she was. He said she had other men friends. He said she put on too much makeup and tried to look sexy."

"Do you believe that, Lisa? I don't think Mom was doing any of those things. Dad was not always right, you know. He was always busy at work or out for drinks with his friends while Mom stayed home with us. She took us to rehearsals at school, piano lessons, and the library. Dad never once did that."

"I remember Dad was always making jokes and telling stories. I don't know why Mom had to get a divorce. Dad never hit her or anything. He just yelled a lot. That's not a reason to get a divorce."

"I always tried to please Dad, and he once called me his dearest girl. I know he loves me—even though he never said it. If we keep trying, maybe we can all live together again."

Noreen shook her head. "I don't want to go back to living with Dad again. He scared me when he got mad and yelled at Mom. His face got red, and he waved his fists in the air like he wanted to hit her. I like it now with just us, Mom, and Sheeba."

"Well, I don't. I'll do all I can to live with Daddy again."

Noreen knew it would never happen, but she did not want to argue with her sister. She always tried to see her sister's side and gave in to her ideas quickly.

A month earlier, Lisa had stepped in at school and chased away three boys who had been intimidating her sister. They had not bothered Noreen again.

Noreen kept quiet and nodded. She loved her big sister.

When the sun was getting past the hills, they turned toward home.

"Did you have a nice walk, Lisa?" her mother asked when they got home.

"It was okay, except that I'm sure I saw that man who moved in down the street. He was hiding behind a tree and watching us. Noreen did not see him, but I did. He scares me, Mom."

Kathy said. "Really? Are you sure?"

"Oh, why ask? You don't believe me anyway." She flounced out of the room, stamping her feet as she went.

*Mathew was peeking at them and hiding behind trees? What a whopper! If Lisa's lies get worse, she'll bring trouble to innocent people.*

# Chapter Four

At the Sunrise Café, Kathy sat and waited for her friend. She had chosen a booth by the window with a good view of the landscape. Tara worked in the finance department at the hospital, but they didn't get together often because their schedules did not jive.

Kathy had known Tara since high school, and they had kept their friendship strong with calls, visits, and e-mails. Tara, though on the plump side, always looked good in outfits that made people take a second look. Her blonde hair was fixed in a ponytail. When she smiled, other people wanted to smile too.

Tara came into the room, and Kathy waved to get her attention. Soon they had ordered and were trying to catch up on past events. Both tried to speak at once and after some laughs they settled down to listen to each other.

"How are things going at home Kathy? Are the girls doing well?

"I am concerned about several things. One is that when they visit their father Lisa is more aggressive and lies more often. The other is that her lying is getting way out of line. She is now accusing our neighbor, the man I told you about, of spying on her. I am at my wit's end."

"That is wild, Kathy. Do you think she might be telling the truth?"

"No. I asked Noreen about it, and she said that she did not see anyone. She was sure that Lisa was making it up."

"What about the new neighbor? I think it's good that you have someone new to talk to. He may turn out to be a special friend, and you need one right now."

"Don't go there, Tara. I have more than enough on my plate right now without some man messing up my head."

"Kathy, you don't need to carry the load all by yourself. Someone to talk to and share ideas with is not messing up anything. He may be just a kind, caring person who might be able to help. You'll never know till you try."

Kathy shook her head. "Thanks, but I can't see anyone helping me with my problems. You're a romantic, Tara, and I have no use for romance just now. How are things going with you, Tara? Are you and George getting along okay? Are there wedding bells in the future?"

"Yes, there are some plans for a wedding in May. George has to wait to see if he gets a promotion in April. If he does, he'll move to New Jersey to work in their Camden office"

"Oh, I will miss you, but if that is where George's job takes him, he has to go. New Jersey should be interesting for you, and New York is close by. Visits there would be great."

All too soon, the lunch was over, and they had to head back to work. As they walked, Tara thought about what to say to Kathy about Lisa. She felt it was best for Lisa to see a child psychiatrist before things got worse.

"Kathy, as your friend and also because I like Lisa, I wish you would reconsider your stand to wait before taking Lisa for help. At least give it some more thought. It won't hurt to check out what is causing these lies, will it?"

"Okay, I will, Tara. I just don't want to make things worse for her. Gossip gets to be hurtful, and I want to protect her as much as I can."

Kathy smiled and waved good-bye to Tara. *She means well and wants to help me. But I can't make a hasty judgment about Lisa. I don't know what thoughts her father is putting into the girl's head, and I can't do anything about that. On top of all that, I can't get Mathew out of my mind. I am so muddled. I am going in circles.*

---

When Kathy got home, there was a message from Mathew on her answering machine.

"Hello, Kathy. This is Mathew calling. I am going to go to a fun thing tonight. I belong to a Big Brother/Sister group, and I sponsor two boys. Timmy is going to play the piano, and Mark is going to sing. There are also jugglers, comics, and more musical talents. Would you and the girls like to come? It starts at seven and is over by eight thirty. I can pick you all up at six thirty if you like. Let me know as soon as you can. My cell phone number is 878-6666. Bye for now."

Kathy smiled and suddenly felt better. She asked Lisa and Noreen if they would like to go.

Noreen said yes, but Lisa only scowled.

Kathy said, "I think it was nice of him to invite us. It sounds like a great program and lots of fun. Get your homework finished, or as much as you can by supper, and we can all go and have a night out."

They were ready on time, and Mathew was a perfect gentleman. He helped each girl into his car and then helped Kathy. He asked about their days and listened as each gave a tidbit of some event of the day.

The gym was crowded, but Mathew had set aside four seats for them earlier that were close to the podium. The children's talents amazed Kathy. Every child did well, and only a few had awkward moments.

Timmy and Mark did their best, and Mathew praised them for how good they sounded. Both children seemed fond of Mathew, and Kathy noticed how they hung on each of his words. They beamed at his praise, and Kathy understood how much it meant to them.

From that night on, Mathew offered outings for the family. First it was a trip to get pumpkins at a farm in Williston. The farm wasn't a large one, but there were horses, a few colts, and a sad-faced goat named Tillie. There also were acres of bright golden pumpkins.

One Saturday, they all went to the Echo Museum by the lake. Twice, they strolled on Church Street and listened to the musicians or were fascinated by the acrobats and jugglers. They also had ice cream at Ben and Jerry's on Church Street.

Halloween was a special treat; Mathew came to the door dressed as a clown. He did somersaults and jigs around the living room. He pulled out treats from an oversized bag that made a noise each time he opened it. Then he put on a movie that was spooky as well as funny. Even Lisa laughed.

Each outing brought Kathy and Mathew closer. Noreen also began to feel at ease with Mathew. He joked with her and seemed to really be interested in her tales from school.

Lisa remained aloof. She still did not like Mathew and often made up stories that Kathy knew were untrue. Her lies were often so weird that Kathy was unsure about when she was telling the truth, bending the truth, or lying.

Thanksgiving was going to be spent without the girls because their father had them for the holiday.

Kathy didn't mind since she would have them for Christmas.

Mathew wondered if Kathy would like to share Thanksgiving with him. He stopped at her house after dinner while he was walking Skipper. He knocked at her door and heard the dog greeting him from inside.

Kathy was surprised to see him and seemed a little flustered. Had she been thinking of him? He hoped so.

"Kathy, I wondered if you would like to share Thanksgiving with me. My mom and dad are both going to be working that day. Dad's a bus driver, and my mom's a nurse. They don't get many holidays off at the same time."

Kathy smiled warmly. She really hadn't looked forward to eating alone. "What can I do to help with dinner?" she asked.

"Just come, and I'll put you to work. I'll even let you help with the dishes!"

Kathy looked forward to being with Mathew, and she fussed over what to wear and how to fix her hair. She decided on dark gray slacks and a mauve sweater. She knew they'd go for a walk after eating and opted for warmth over elegance. She slid into her practical walking shoes with a sigh.

When she arrived, Mathew was getting the turkey breast ready for the oven. He asked her to help with the dressing. She also cut up broccoli and fixed the potatoes for baking.

The day was cold but sunny, and they took the dogs for a long walk before going back to Mathew's house to finish cooking the dinner. As they walked, Mathew took Kathy's hand in his.

Kathy decided to live in the moment, letting the warmth of Mathew fill her with contentment. It felt so good to be close to him, so right.

Kathy had brought some fruity white wine that was not too sweet. It went well with the turkey breast and the veggies Mathew had provided. There was a pumpkin pie and whipped cream for the topping.

"You are spoiling me," Kathy said as she looked over the feast on the table. "You had better let me help with cleaning up. I don't want to feel useless."

"Okay, you can help. We can share the work. And then would you like to play gin rummy, listen to music, or watch TV?"

"Oh, I bet you play a mean gin rummy game. But I think I am better. Get ready to lose, big boy." She tried to hide a grin. She was an expert at the game.

"Ha! We'll see. I think I can wipe that smirk off your face, and you'll eat crow."

When the kitchen was clean, they sat at the kitchen table and shuffled the cards. Lisa took the first turn, but Mathew won in a tough fight. After several more games, which Mathew won easily, Kathy called it quits. "I surrender. You are the best player I have ever met."

Mathew rose and pulled Kathy to her feet. "Did I tell you there was going to be a penalty for the loser?"

He took her face in his hands, and to a surprised Kathy, kissed her gently but thoroughly.

She didn't pull away. A warm tingling swept down her, turning her limp and more than eager. She placed her arms around Mathew's neck and gently brought them closer. Mathew needed no more encouragement and deepened the kiss. His hands roamed up and down her back. He finally pulled her closer, and she could feel his erection pulsing against her.

Finally, Mathew gently drew away. He wanted more, much more, but he knew it was too soon. She'd had enough of a bad relationship and didn't need one that could go nowhere anytime soon.

He drew her to the sofa and sat her close to him. He put his arms around her and said in an unsteady voice, "I didn't mean for that to go beyond a friendly kiss. I got carried away. It won't happen again, Kathy. I know you have enough to worry about without me taking advantage of you. Please forgive me."

Kathy was shaken. *Wasn't the kiss good for him too? Didn't he feel the same way? His erection proved that he was eager for more. What happened? He had meant it to be a friendly kiss? Impossible! I had better stay away from him in the future if I react to his kiss this way. I have been without someone to love me for too long. But then again, Bruce never loved me—he just used me.*

Kathy looked into Mathew's eyes. They were warm and caring. He had been thinking of her. She grinned and quickly said, "The kiss was super, and I did have to pay the penalty, didn't I? How about taking the dogs for a walk before I go home? It is cold, but the moon is out. There's no snow yet."

Mathew went to get their coats, hats, and mittens. The dogs were happy to be going out again, and they leaped about like puppies.

Later, as she snuggled in her blue flannel nightgown, Kathy thought of how nice it would be to have Mathew beside her, hugging her close. *His kiss was really something. I think he would be a fantastic lover.* She felt warmth from her face to her toes, and it was coupled with an intense longing. *Could it be possible? Forget it, girl. It will never happen.*

# Chapter Five

November brought cold weather but no snow. Kathy and the girls all had cross-country skis, and they watched the weather forecast each day, hoping for snow. Nearby, there were several good places for cross-country skiing. They could take a picnic or have lunch at a nearby deli.

Friday evening was bitterly cold, and there was a smell of snow in the air.

"If it snows tonight, Mom, can we go skiing?" Noreen pleaded.

"Well, if we can get some of the laundry done and the housework finished, we might be able to go after lunch."

Noreen was excited. "How can I help, Mom? I know how to put the clothes into the washer, and I can dust for you."

"How about you, Lisa? Can you give a hand?"

Lisa replied, "I suppose."

"Great," Kathy said. "We can hope for snow and get up early to do the chores."

Both girls seemed ready to help, and Kathy said a silent prayer of thanks. *I wonder if Mathew likes to ski.*

*It would be more fun if he went with us. I think I'll ask him to come along. He's invited us to many events lately, and it won't be like I am being pushy. Well, perhaps I am, but I like him. He's good company.*

When she had the dishes cleared away, she called Mathew. She told him of their plans to go cross-country skiing. He agreed to go along and offered to drive; his Subaru could hold all the skis and gear. When she told the girls that Mathew would be coming with them, Noreen was happy, but Lisa made a face and sighed.

Saturday morning held gray skies, and the ground was covered with three or four inches of new snow. The morning was busy before they left for the ski area. Kathy wore her winter parka and her cherry red hat.

Mathew helped load all the skis into his car. Kathy couldn't help but admire his steady stride, the way he packed the skis so easily, and his warm smile. His eagerness to enjoy life was lifting her spirits.

He turned to Kathy. "Like what you see?" He said with a wink. Her face was almost as red as her ski hat, but she winked before turning away.

The sun was shining, and the reflection on the snow was like diamonds glittering all around. "What a beautiful day," said Kathy. "It isn't too cold, and I am looking forward to cross country skiing. I call it skating on the snow. I'm glad you could come with us, Mathew. Have you skied much? Do you like cross-country skiing?"

"I always liked to ski, Kathy. I even taught skiing at a ski school when I was younger."

Soon they were on their skis, sliding over the snow and feeling the lift of being outdoors. It was not too crowded, and the afternoon sped by.

Mathew heard Lisa cry out and raced over to see if he could help. She was rubbing her ankle as if she had twisted it. Mathew leaned down to check her ankle and leg, but she pushed him away.

"I'll be okay in a minute. Just let me get my breath." After a few minutes, Lisa got up and caught up with Kathy and Noreen.

Mathew watched her ski away. *Well, so much for thanks. Lisa has some problems, but she also has great potential. She is a gifted artist, and her sketches are finely drawn. Her science projects are always well done, as she puts all her energy into them. However, her problems run deep, and she needs a kind, but firmer hand. I'm sure a good psychiatrist would make a difference. I wonder why Kathy's so stubborn about this. Can't she see that Lisa's in trouble?*

---

The next weekend, the girls visited their father. Mathew and Kathy went cross-country skiing again. They also had dinner on Church Street.

Kathy was quiet at dinner, and Mathew asked what was wrong.

"Oh, there's nothing special. I just get the feeling that the girls will come home believing Bruce's lies about me. He fills their heads with his tales of what I have done wrong and how bad a mother I am. Noreen does not seem to be affected, but Lisa seems to believe his every word. He still resents the divorce, and he tries to get back at me through the girls. I don't know what I can do about it. I don't want to keep them away from their father. He has a right see them. When they come back, Lisa is sullen and hard to manage. She believes that if she agrees with her father, we can all go back to living together again. She forgets what it was like or is in denial."

Mathew sat and thought for a moment. "I think one way is to go to the judge that made the decision about their visits to their dad. You could ask for a review of that decision and for supervised visits. I don't know if it would be granted, but it's worth a try. Do you think their father is saying things to make Lisa unhappy at home? Perhaps there is another reason that we haven't thought of."

"Thanks, Mathew. I did not even think about that. There may be something else, but I still think asking for supervised visits would be helpful. He would be furious, but it may stop him from upsetting the children. I will make an appointment to see the judge soon."

"That sounds good, Kathy. Just try to be open to the idea that Lisa has problems—and her father may or may not be a cause."

Kathy nodded. He was right. She had a habit of jumping to conclusions and then hanging on to it. *I often put things aside to think about later, and then I don't follow through. I know it is one of my bad habits.*

"What do you do at Christmas, Kathy? Do you have a tree? Do you go to church on Christmas Eve? Do you make a special dinner for your family?"

"I have the girls for the Christmas holidays. My work is flexible, and I can get time off to be with them. I make a special dinner, and we have a tree and presents. How about you? What are your plans?"

"I usually go home to my parents' house for the day, but this year they are going to San Francisco. My brother and his wife live there with their three children. They try to go there every other year. They will be visiting me in a few weeks, and I want you to meet them."

"If you are going to be alone, Mathew, why don't you plan to have Christmas with us? My parents will be here too."

"I'd like that, Kathy. Thanks for the invitation. I'd like to bring something to add to the day. How about some wine? I can also make a special Christmas cake that has a great hard sauce to go with it."

"That sounds yummy. I never had that dessert before. What is it called?"

"It is an English dessert called figgy pudding. In case someone doesn't like the pudding, I will also make a pumpkin pie."

"Wow! What talent you have. I am impressed."

Mathew almost blushed, and he slyly said, "I have other talents too." He wished he hadn't been so bold, but the words just skipped out.

Kathy saw how he felt and giggled. "Like to brag, do we?"

Mathew said, "Well, there's skiing, baking, helping trim Christmas trees, and lots more."

Kathy had to laugh at his list. She wondered if kissing or being a good lover was also on it, but she chased the thought away. It wasn't the right time to think about that when she had Lisa and her problems to worry her, but the thoughts kept intruding.

# Chapter Six

On Sunday evening, the girls came home from their visit with their father.

Lisa went right to bed without saying more than hello to her mother. Noreen, on the other hand, was full of her visit. She said her father was going to get them something special for Christmas. He didn't say what, but he had hinted it was a huge surprise.

Kathy wondered what he was going to give them, but she had no way to know if it would be a good thing for the girls or not.

Noreen said, "He said that you would probably not like it, but he was going to do it anyway."

Kathy wondered what he was thinking of, but since there were four more weeks until Christmas, she felt it was best not to worry. She wished they could work together for the good of the girls. Bruce had never consulted her about anything. He liked to be in control. *I wonder if he is aware of how often Lisa lies.* They hadn't talked for a while since every time she tried to speak to him about the girls, he became defensive. *I know he speaks ill of me. Noreen told me so—and she doesn't lie. I must remember to call the judge and ask for a review of their visiting agreement. There must be something going on at Bruce's house that upsets Lisa.*

Kathy knew she'd have to be specific about why she wanted the rules changed. She wrote some of her concerns on a piece of paper. When she finished, she sat at the kitchen table for a while and thought about her dinner with Mathew. She forgot to put the paper away before she went to bed.

The next morning, Lisa found the paper on the table. She picked it up and read it over and over. *Mom is going to have someone there when we visit Dad. Also, she does not want us to stay over at his house. Dad's right. She is mean. I'm going to call Dad and tell him what I found.* She remembered that her dad went to work early, and it was already eight o'clock. *I'll call him tonight. He'll fix her.*

⸺⬥⬥⸺

When Kathy came into the kitchen the next morning, the paper had been moved. *I'll bet Lisa read this. Well, that can't be changed now. I have to do what's right—even if the girls are upset.*

Kathy's request to meet with the judge had been granted within a week. Kathy hurried up the steps of the courthouse to keep her appointment with Judge Hervey. As usual, he was prompt and listened to her plea for a review.

He said, "Mrs. Hilliard, your daughter has always been likely to lie. Do you think her father is abetting that?"

"Yes. It is quite possible. Both girls are always upset when they come home, Lisa more than Noreen. I am certain the visits are the cause—especially for Lisa. He keeps trying to get the children back by making up stories about me. He believes that if he gets the children on his side, we can get back together again. What can I do to change this? He has hinted to the girls that he will take them to Disney World soon. He has no legal right to do that without my approval. And it's wrong to get the girls excited about a trip that cannot happen."

"Now let me be clear about this, Mrs. Hilliard. You want to limit visits to their dad to daytime only, and they must be supervised."

"Yes, Judge Harvey. And make certain he understands that no trips out of town are acceptable without our mutual agreement. He only got every other weekend and no trips out of town because of his aggressive behavior."

The judge said, "I can't change their visits to their dad without more collaboration. Let me talk to the social worker about this to see if she can find out more. It will take her a while to find out the facts, but if I find that he is causing them stress, I will certainly do my best to change the way they visit him. Let me give this some more thought, and I will get in touch with you in a few weeks. It has to be a legal draft and not a phone call. I will think about this most carefully before I make a decision. It may take several weeks before I can finalize it. This is a serious decision, and I want to be fair. The children's welfare comes first, as you know."

❈

After several weeks, Judge Harvey called and said a letter was going out to the girl's father. When she received her copy, she read it. "Beginning on December 20, the time and duration of visits of Lisa and Noreen Hilliard to their father, Bruce Hilliard, will be as follows: Only daytime visits will be permitted. Each visit will be supervised by someone trained to do this. Her name is Mrs. Geraldine Cassidy. Any violation of this ruling would endanger all future visits, and they could be terminated at the court's request."

Kathy sighed with relief. *One hurdle crossed. Now if I can only get Lisa to be truthful—what a miracle that would be.*

❈

Work was busy for Kathy. Winter brought colds and flu. Many more people came to the hospital with winter health issues. She was beginning to become stressed, and time was getting short for Christmas shopping. She made lists and then forgot them, and she had no time to shop anyway. Just getting to and from work, keeping things going at home, and taking care of Lisa and Noreen was a challenge.

Mathew called several times, but Kathy couldn't take time to go out or go skiing. They made a final plan for Christmas week. He offered to help her get a tree and put it up. Everyone would help decorate it.

The weekend before Christmas, Mathew came to the door early to pick out the tree. He insisted that the girls come too, and he wanted to buy one special box of Christmas ornaments for each girl.

It was a cloudy, cold day, but they took their time. They chose a live tree that smelled good. Kathy liked to have a live one when possible. Mathew bought a new tree stand that he claimed would save time. Even the girls seemed to enjoy the outing.

When they arrived home, Kathy made hot chocolate for them all and brought out some chocolate chip cookies to go with it.

"You sure make the best cookies, Kathy. My mother made these when I was little. It is one of the things I miss."

"Oh, Mathew, take some home when you go. I have lots more in the freezer. I make them in huge batches, and there are plenty."

Mathew and Kathy put the tree up near the window in the living room. It was really impressive— and the room was filled with its woodsy scent. They all took turns trimming the tree. Lisa and Noreen added the ornaments that Mathew had given them. Kathy looked at Mathew and saw such love and yearning that she trembled deep inside.

Noreen and Lisa went to the kitchen to put away the cookies and clean up.

"You know what I forgot?" Mathew asked.

"What?"

"Mistletoe!"

He came closer and grinned. "I can't kiss you without some mistletoe, can I?"

Kathy did not answer, but she didn't back away either.

Mathew took her hand and gently brought her closer. His lips were gentle, and she was startled by the intense yearning that washed over her. It began with his touch, and a wave of need made her gasp. He deepened the kiss, and they both forgot everything but the wonderful sensations they were feeling.

Voices from the kitchen jolted them apart, and Kathy jumped back.

Mathew shook his head. "I shouldn't have done that, Kathy. I have wanted to for a long time, but I know that now is not the best time. I just couldn't help myself."

"Are you saying you're sorry you kissed me?" she asked. "Well, that kiss was awesome, and I thank you for our second kiss. Do you think we need a little more practice?"

Mathew needed no more invitation. He was more than willing to practice. Finally she gasped and pulled away, shaken and aware of her heart racing.

He gently pulled her closer and held her.

She could feel his erection pressed up against her, letting her know of his desire.

"Oh, Kathy, you'll never know how much I ache for you." He ran his hands up and down her back, soothing her and causing her to want more. "I'd better go before I make a complete idiot of myself. I know this is too soon. Can we still be friends? I want to keep on seeing you. Let's give it some time. You have to get to know me better, and the girls have to accept me too. Is that okay with you?"

She wanted to say no, but she knew he was right. "Of course we can be friends. The girls may take a little time before accepting you, especially Lisa. However, I think she will come to see how special you are—and how much you mean to me."

Mathew held her close and tried to reassure her that all would turn out okay. He gave her a final kiss and reluctantly went home.

---

On the day before Christmas, Kathy called and invited Mathew to meet her parents. They had just arrived from Richmond, Vermont. They would only be staying two nights, and Kathy was anxious to have them all meet. She hoped they would like

Mathew—and that Lisa would be at her best. She had baked some extra cookies and a loaf of date nut bread, which was her father's favorite.

Mathew opened Kathy's door and called, "Hello."

A petite, gray-haired lady smiled and said, "Kathy's in the den with her father just now, and she asked me to welcome you. I'm Diane Hilliard, Kathy's mother. You must be Mathew. I've heard so much about you. Kathy's so happy to have you as a neighbor."

He took off his coat, hat, and boots and sat in the living room. Noreen came in and greeted him with a hug. Lisa smiled and sat down on a chair by the fireplace.

Kathy's father was a tall, slightly bald man. Jeffrey wore a plaid flannel shirt and dark tan slacks. His hair and short beard were gray. His handshake was firm, and his smile lit up his weathered face. Kathy's parents were both warm and outgoing.

Mathew soon felt at ease. Mrs. Hilliard had her arm around Lisa's shoulders, trying to help her relax. Mrs. Hilliard and Lisa were deep in a conversation about pencils, charcoal, and the animals that were easiest to draw.

Kathy brought in some drinks and Christmas cookies.

Noreen listened to the chatter around her and devoured the cookies.

Kathy teased Mathew about his talents.

Jeffrey said, "I often help Diane do dishes and laundry."

After wishing them all a good night, Mathew said. "I'll be up early to see you open the presents. Don't do anything till I get here, okay? He heard some giggles and words he could not hear clearly as he closed the door and trudged up the snowy road toward home.

❖

Kathy was up at dawn and made a big pot of coffee. She opened the door for Mathew, and they had a few quiet moments before the girls came down. She snuggled into his arms with a sigh.

He rubbed her back and was about to slip his hands under her sweater when he realized what he was doing. He stepped away with an apologetic smile. "I can't help it, but I want to touch you, Kathy. Please forgive me. I'll try to curb my wants."

Noreen and Lisa stumbled down the stairs, sat on the floor sleepily, and waited for Kathy's mother and father to join them.

When they were all settled, Mathew gave Lisa her gift.

She squealed in delight when she opened the set of watercolors, brushes, and paper. Sketching and painting were her favorite pastimes, and she was very good for her age. There was also a book of sketches and watercolor instructions.

When Lisa saw the bright red bicycle, she was speechless for a moment. "Is this from Daddy?" When she found out it was from Mathew, her face went pale. There was a helmet too. She stammered her thanks.

"I think it will be a good fit, Lisa," Mathew said. "And I can help you to learn to ride it if you want."

Lisa nodded and gave him a vague smile.

Noreen's gift was a box of various games. She also opened a smaller box with a bracelet of natural stones. "Oh, how lovely." She smiled at Mathew and thanked him, almost stammering in her shyness.

Mathew also gave both girls a gift certificate to a large department store.

Kathy was happy that he had been so generous. Both girls needed new winter boots. Kathy hid a smile when she overheard Lisa say, "I'm going to get a new training bra and a nightgown from Victoria's Secret when we go to the mall."

Mathew gave Kathy a sky-blue cashmere sweater and a gift certificate to a flower shop on Church Street. There were also packages for Diane and Jeffrey and goofy toys for Skipper and Sheeba.

Kathy gave a leather wallet and several books to Mathew. The books were thrillers by an author he liked. When the gift exchanges were over, Kathy made some hot chocolate for Lisa and Noreen and coffee for the adults.

Mathew went home to feed Skipper and take him for his morning walk.

Kathy was determined to fix the best dinner ever, and she quickly began to make stuffing and get the turkey ready for the oven. The veggies were washed and put in the fridge for later. Mathew's figgy pudding and sauce were on the counter. He had also brought a large pumpkin pie with whipped cream for a topping.

Kathy looked at the large dining table. Noreen and Lisa had set the table with Kathy's best china and fancy linen napkins. A poinsettia graced the center, and there were two candles on each side. Kathy beamed at them. "Thank you. You both have done a professional job. The table looks elegant."

While the turkey cooked, they all played an easy card game. Noreen won and jumped up and down, elated over her win. Mathew came back and joined the games. Kathy looked at the happy group. She thought about how nice it was to all get along. *This is how a family should be—not the way it was with Bruce.*

The feast was as perfect as Kathy had planned. Her dad said the grace. She felt warm and happy as she looked around the table.

Noreen put some Christmas music on the stereo, and the songs of the season added to the pleasant harmony.

Mathew and Kathy's eyes met across the table. Both saw the happiness in each other's eyes.

Mathew lifted his glass of wine. "Thanks for a wonderful Christmas, Kathy, Noreen, and Lisa.

It's one of the nicest I've had in years. Meeting you, Diane and Jeffrey, made it even more special."

A quiet contentment settled over the table. Kathy hoped it was a sign of harmony in the future. Like a child, she crossed he fingers under the table and hoped her Christmas wish would come true.

# Chapter Seven

January and February brought snow and icy roads. Kathy and Mathew spent each Saturday together, sometimes at his house and often at hers. When the girls had the weekend with her, they were all together. They watched TV, made popcorn, and watched movies. If the roads weren't too bad, they drove to the cross-country ski park.

Mathew often offered to help Lisa with her schoolwork or projects that needed a little advice, but she usually declined. Noreen became closer to Mathew even as Lisa coldly kept her distance. Nothing that Mathew did could change Lisa's mind.

He felt her anger at him and attributed it to feelings of separation from her dad. She still visited her father every other weekend, but she did not stay overnight. Once he overheard her arguing with Noreen about how her father was going to make her mom sorry she got a divorce. Lisa was old enough to understand, but she didn't want to give up her dream of living with her dad and her mother again.

Mathew told Kathy about hearing this, and she said she thought it would pass with time. Mathew was not so sure. He wondered what had happened to Kathy's plan to take Lisa to a psychiatrist. He sighed. *She really is being stubborn about this. It isn't doing Lisa any good to wait.*

Mathew's mother and father came for a visit in February. They stayed for several days, inviting Kathy and the girls to have dinner with them and charming everyone with their easygoing conversation. Even Lisa seemed to enjoy their company—as well as Mathew's mom's little cakes. They were from an old German recipe. They were filled with honey, almonds, and fat raisins.

Kathy thought Shirley and Ralph Kennedy had welcomed Kathy as though they understood Mathew cared for her and she would be a part of their life.

Was she fantasizing? Did they really care about her and her daughters? Kathy had a warm feeling inside for weeks after they had gone home. Pennsylvania was not so far away, and they had promised to keep in touch and visit again soon.

---

Mathew knocked at Kathy's door and said, "Kathy, there's a Saint Patrick's Day dinner with music on the big day. It's right here in town at your favorite restaurant. How about getting a sitter and going with me to hear the band and eat some good traditional corned beef and cabbage?"

"That sounds lovely, Mathew. We haven't gone out too much since it has been so cold and icy. I even have a green dress to wear."

When he hugged her, he thought he heard Lisa say, "Oh, geez." He looked up, but no one was near. *I am getting tired of catering to that child. She still lies when she wants to get attention or make things go her way. She is hard to understand most of the time. I wish Kathy would do what is really good for Lisa and take her to get some help. I do my best, but my hands are tied. Kathy is in denial here. I'm going to get her a list of some well-recommended psychologists that specialize in children's problems. She has to stop putting this off.* He held Kathy for a moment longer, then said. "Who can you get to stay with the girls while we go out for dinner and music?"

Kathy thought a moment and remembered a friend who had retired in August. She had offered to stay with Noreen and Lisa if needed. "I know of someone I can call. If Paula's not too busy, she will be perfect."

"Great. I will make reservations as soon as you know."

---

Noreen was trying to draw a picture in her room. She had sketched a house with a barn and fencing, but she needed to put in some trees, bushes, and a horse or two. She looked up as Lisa came into the room.

"Hi, Lisa. Take a look at my drawing. Do you think it's any good?"

Lisa came closer and saw what Noreen had sketched. "Oh, this is nice, Noreen. You really are getting good at this. Have you seen my latest paintings? Everyone says I am really talented."

Noreen gasped. She knew that everyone said Lisa was an excellent artist for her age, but she didn't have to be so mean about it.

"You are getting better, Noreen, but I know I am really good. I did some new drawings a while ago. I knew you'd be jealous; that's why I didn't show them to you."

Noreen began to cry. She rubbed her eyes, but the tears still flowed. She knew her sister was acting mean because she was upset about something. She didn't know just what it was. *Why does Lisa do this? She takes her anger out on me.* She would get over it, but it still hurt.

"Oh stop crying, Noreen. I came in to tell you what I overheard just now. Mom and Mathew are going to go out for a whole evening. We'll be alone, except for some old lady who'll be with us. When they are gone, we can call Dad and have a long, private talk with him. I'm going to tell him about how close Mathew is getting to Mom. He's always hugging or kissing her. I think he plans to marry her and then he'll be here night and day—forever."

Noreen wiped her eyes on her sleeve. "Why do you hate him, Lisa? He has been good to us; he has taken us skiing and bought us nice lunches. He only wants to be a part of our family. You make up stories about him and tell the kids at school that he is mean and nasty. I wish you wouldn't lie about him like that."

"I thought you were my sister and cared for me," Lisa yelled. "Don't you see what he's doing? If Mom marries him, we will never be back with Dad again. I hate him. I wish he were dead. I do."

Lisa stormed out of Noreen's room and stomped down the hall. Lisa's door crashed shut.

Noreen finally stopped crying. She bit her nails, worrying about the hate she heard in Lisa's voice. She was sorry for Lisa—but frightened too. Lisa's hatred scared her.

❧

When March arrived, it brought sleet and more cold weather. By St. Patrick's Day, the weather had abated, and a cool but sunny day brought the hope of spring closer. Paula had agreed to stay with the girls, and Kathy was anticipating the evening.

Kathy looked in the mirror with a critical eye. She felt the green dress made her eyes look larger, and the color complemented her skin. She checked her makeup and her nylons again. It would have to do; Mathew was waiting.

Mathew had brought a new video for Lisa and Noreen to watch. He knew it would be a hit since they had mentioned it several times. They both thanked him, but Lisa smirked as if she had a secret.

When Kathy entered the living room, Mathew said, "Oh, you are just beautiful. The color of that dress makes you look like an Irish fairy. I can't wait to dance with you. I will be the envy of all the men there."

Kathy felt like a princess and grinned at him. She nodded her head and said, "You're not too bad yourself." He looked great in his dark blue suit. He wore a light green shirt and a dark green tie.

Mathew said, "I think we're a great pair."

After saying good-bye to Paula and the girls, he took her arm. They went out to his car, and he tenderly helped her into her seat. Soon, they were on their way.

The evening was perfect. The dinner of traditional corned beef and cabbage was excellent. With it, they had several glasses of ice-cold lager. Later, they danced most of the dances. They sat at a table for six, and the other couples were good company. When it was eleven thirty, they were reluctant to leave, but they had promised Paula to be back by twelve thirty.

Halfway home, Mathew stopped the car and sat still for a moment.

"What is it, Mathew?"

"Kathy, I've waited a long time for things to be 'just right' before asking you this. But I think the time will never be just right. I hope Lisa will soon begin to like me, but I won't count on it. So that leaves us with one question—will you marry me and hope for the best?"

Kathy wasn't surprised. She had hoped Mathew would love her enough to ask her to be his wife, but she had reservations because of Lisa. She yearned to share their lives together. She felt his love every time he did some thoughtful thing for her or the girls. He had kept his emotions in check because of her and her situation. *But I too am tired of waiting to be happy. I love him with all my heart. He is so different from Bruce, and he loves the girls as well as me.*

Kathy didn't realize how long she was quiet.

Mathew asked, "Is it too hard to say yes?"

"Oh, Mathew. Yes! Yes! I was thinking of how much I love you and hoping that Lisa will not be a problem for long." She turned into his arms and held him close as he kissed her.

At first, it was a gentle kiss, just a taste of her. Then they both exploded, and heat coursed through them, connecting then in a flame of desire. His hands touched every part of her that he could reach. She was also busy finding a way to get under his coat.

"Let's go to my house for a while," Mathew said.

Kathy nodded and kept her hand on his thigh as they drove the rest of the way. The drive was short, and Kathy was shivering with anticipation.

As soon as they were in Mathew's bedroom, they yanked off their clothes as fast as they could. Kathy was at fever pitch, and Skip was more than ready.

Mathew turned down the sheets, and they lay down. His gaze feasted on her hair and face and then her rounded breasts. Inch by inch, he caressed her with his eyes.

*God, she is beautiful.* "Kathy, you are so lovely. I want to love every inch of you."

He started with little kisses that made her gasp with pleasure. His hands brought a moan as he found her erotic spots. He followed with his lips, and his tender kisses brought her almost to a climax.

"Oh, no, I'm going to have my turn too." Kathy's fingers began to read him as if he were Braille. From one erotic spot to another, she stroked and kissed him.

He was shaking with need, but he was trying to prolong it as long as possible. He groaned, "I can't hold out much longer. You're killing me."

He rolled her over and was soon rubbing and coaxing her to give him entry. She opened her legs wider as she lifted herself toward him. He joined her to him with a gentle thrust. Gradually, his pace increased.

Kathy held him close and rubbed his shoulders in mindless pleasure. He soon climaxed, and his whole body trembled and shook. He was glad they were alone; his yell would have awakened the dead.

He knew Kathy hadn't reached her climax; in seconds, his hands caressed her tender, full breasts and gradually moved down. His lips moved down to her navel, kissing her soft skin as he slowly sought her warm nest. She jumped as his lips found the soft folds, and she moaned and thrashed her head back and forth as she neared her climax. With a scream of release, she shuddered with vibrations that rocked her to her core.

Mathew held her as she trembled, reliving the rapture they had shared.

---

When it was time to go home, Kathy did her best to quiet her racing heart and tried to smooth her hair. She could feel her swollen lips and was sure her wrinkled dress would give them away. She hoped her smile was genuine as she opened the door to greet Paula.

Paula said, "I was getting worried. It is well after one o'clock, and I thought something may have happened to you."

"Paula, I'm sorry to be so late. We have just become engaged, and we had to celebrate."

Paula squealed with joy. "That's the nicest news I've heard in a while. I wish you every joy. You both deserve to be happy."

Mathew offered to drive Paula home since it was so late, but she refused. She said she would be fine. He insisted and would not listen to her "It is not far, and I will feel better knowing you are home safe."

Mathew kissed Kathy good-bye and said, "I don't want to stay here overnight until we are married. It would not be the best idea, considering the girls."

Kathy couldn't sleep. She tossed and turned most of the night, praying that she had done the right thing. Lisa was not going to be happy about the news. She still thought they could all be family again if Mathew went away.

*Oh, I wish I knew the right thing to do. I have made an appointment with Dr. Jane Silverman at the health clinic. I know Lisa's lying is out of control, and she needs help. I want to do my best for her, but shouldn't Mathew and I have some happiness? I've been alone so long.*

With thoughts racing around in her head, Kathy was still awake at six. She groggily went to take a shower before the girls were up.

Breakfast was almost over before Kathy had a chance to share her news. The girls were going to their father's for the weekend, but they would come home to sleep. It wasn't the best time to tell them the plans, but there would never be a best time. She looked at them and said, "Don't go yet. I have something to tell you."

The girls looked up and waited as she took another deep breath.

"Last night, Mathew asked me to marry him—and I said yes. I know it will mean big changes for all of us, but he is a good man and loves me as much as I love him. We want to be together as one family. I know he cares for you both. I hope you will do your best to help make this happen."

Noreen smiled and said, "Mom, I like him a lot. He has shown us many good times and has taken us skiing and out to nice places to eat. He made our Christmas special. He makes me laugh too."

Lisa's face was white and she sat very still. Finally, she shouted, "I don't believe it! We don't want to have him in our house. We only have one dad, and we would all be together if you hadn't left him. I don't want him as a friend or a stepdad. He is not a good person. Dad told me so."

Kathy felt as if someone had kicked her in the belly. She gasped and couldn't think of a word to say. She opened her mouth to speak, but then she closed it again. *What in the world has gotten into this child? Why did she react so differently than Noreen did? Was her dad making her angry with his lies about me? Oh, God what should I do?*

"Lisa, I know your father has given you ideas that cannot be true. Your father does not know Mathew. He has never met him; how can he say anything about him? You must learn to think for yourself. Mathew has been very kind to all of us. Remember the times he has helped you with your science projects and other homework, taken us on outings, or out to fine restaurants? I can't see how you can believe your father's mean and untrue remarks. He is lying out of spite and a need for revenge. He is angry because I now have love in my life. Mathew is a kind, caring man."

"I hate him! I'll never call him 'Dad' or even talk to him. If you marry him, you'll be sorry. He is not what you think he is. Dad found out a lot about him, and I believe him." She stormed out of the room, went to her room, and slammed the door.

Kathy sat at the table, shaking as if she would break apart. *What is wrong with that girl? How can I marry Mathew when we will be always shouting at each other with cruel, angry words?*

Noreen said, "Don't cry Mom. Lisa will be okay after a while. It's something new, and she is being mean. She'll be okay."

Somehow, Kathy doubted it.

❦

On Monday, Kathy called the psychiatrist and reconfirmed Lisa's appointment. She told the physician about her daughter and the scene after Lisa was told about her decision to marry Mathew. She was reassured by Dr. Silverman's professional attitude and the confidentiality of the meetings.

She called Mathew and told him she had to see him pronto. He said he would see her that evening after the girls were settled for the night. She had to try hard to keep her spirits up and not let her coworkers see how worried she was. It was an effort, but it was worthwhile. The day passed without any problems or need to explain.

When the girls had said their goodnights, she turned the lights low and waited for Mathew. He tapped softly at the back door, and she almost fell into his arms with relief.

He held her close and rubbed her back. Then he showered her with tiny kisses that almost made her forget what she had to tell him. Finally, with a huge sigh, she made him sit at the kitchen table. She poured them both a glass of white wine and sat down across from him.

Mathew raised his eyebrows and said, "What is it, Kathy? What is so wrong that you can't even tell me?"

"It's Lisa again. She hit the ceiling when I told her about our marriage plans. She was hysterical and screamed that she would never live with us and that she hated you. I just don't see how we can all be together if she continues to be so upset."

Mathew was quiet. His shoulders shook, and he looked as if he would explode. Finally he grew still and shook his head to clear it. "I don't know what to say, Kathy. This is not a surprise, but she is more upset than I imagined she would be. She seems unhinged and unable to think straight. She must come first, of course—but for how long? We have to help her regain her composure and ease her fears before we can do anything. Perhaps it would be a good idea to let Lisa live with her father. She and her dad could also have visits with the child psychiatrist."

"I don't know if Bruce is stable either, Mathew. They come back from his home sullen and unmanageable. Lisa would be happy at first, but we need to find the underlying problem that's making her so difficult. It would be a stopgap measure. Also, once she is back with her dad, it would be hard to change again. I think going for visits with Dr. Silverman first and then listening to her advice is the best idea for now." Kathy stood and walked to his side. She put her arms around him and cradled his head in her arms. "Skip, you are so caring and kind. You give me hope that all will work out for us. I hope the doctor can bring about a miracle. Then Lisa can be a normal girl who can let her fears go and accept our love for each other and for her and Noreen."

Mathew nodded. He drew her closer and gently rubbed her back He lifted her onto his lap and held her close. He caressed her with loving hands. His strokes eased her tight muscles. His lips covered hers with a gentle kiss that deepened and sent warm waves of longing racing to her very core.

"Please come back to my house with me, Kathy. This is not the right place for us to be together. One of the girls might wake up."

Kathy nodded and called her neighbor to ask if she would keep an eye on her house for about an hour. They drove to Mathew's house and tiptoed into the living room. They undressed each other frantically.

Kathy spread a plaid throw on the rug before the fireplace. There were still some embers glowing, and it was almost like magic to feel the warmth on her skin. He was so warm and strong. She reveled in his touch and closeness.

They touched and stroked each other. His kisses brought her to the peak of need.

She whispered, "Yes, yes."

He took his time, stroking her breasts and caressing her.

With a soft cry, Kathy climaxed. She shuddered as waves of pleasure rippled over her.

Kathy's hands began to caress him, and her nails gently stroked his back. She tightened and released her inner muscles.

Mathew shook, and he came with a loud cry that was almost primeval. Intense vibrations shook his body. He'd never had an experience like this before. The difference, he thought, was love.

She held him as he quivered, each sensation fading in a pleasant slow return to peace. They finally rose and dressed without speaking.

In the kitchen, Mathew made a fresh pot of coffee. They sipped the brew while pondering their situation.

Kathy's thoughts were bleak, and her mind went around in circles. She felt hopeless. Kathy put her hands over Mathew's hands, and they looked at one another for a long moment, each offering love and hope.

A feeling of peace came over Kathy as she held his hand. *Somehow it will all work out. It just has to.*

Mathew sighed and said. "We have to postpone our wedding until Lisa can accept me. I hope Dr. Silverman can help Lisa. She has to get over this lying. I want her to become mature so she can be the person she is meant to be."

Kathy looked at him and said, "I know you're right, and I am happy that you are willing to wait. I never thought I'd see the day that I'd feel so much pain about Lisa's behavior. Perhaps Dr. Silverman can give us a miracle."

<hr />

When the girls came home from their visit to their father, Kathy sat them both down at the kitchen table. She pinned them with a stern look and said, "I think you owe me an apology, Lisa. That outburst at breakfast was uncalled for. Mathew has been kind to all of us. You are letting your father put some ugly ideas in your head. And Noreen, you should not let Lisa continue to hurt you. Yes, I know she does that, and you are not helping her by putting up with it. From now on, there will be consequences for any lies, bullying, or angry outbursts. Do you understand me?"

Lisa nodded, but her sullen expression gave Kathy pause.

"I mean it, Lisa. You are out of control. Don't hurt Noreen's feelings just because you are unhappy.

Why don't you count the good things about Mathew instead of trying to make him out to be a villain? Your father is wrong to lie to you about Mathew. So, no more of that—do you hear?"

The girls were silent as they went up to bed.

Kathy heard Noreen's door shut and Lisa's slam. She poured a glass of white wine and sipped it as she gazed out the window. *What have I done wrong? How could I have not seen how unstable Lisa is? Everyone warned me about Lisa's lies, but I haven't paid enough attention. I haven't done enough to curb Lisa's behavior. I should not have let her lying slide by.* Tears slowly rolled down her face as she watched her dreams crumbling to dust.

# Chapter Eight

The next morning, Lisa was quiet at breakfast. She took her school bag, went to the door, and said, "Bye, Mom."

Kathy wondered about that all day at work. *What had happened at her father's house on Sunday?* Lisa seemed to be in another world. She was quiet, but she had an odd look on her face.

After school, Lisa said she would walk down to the lake. She was gone longer than Kathy thought she should be. Lisa usually came home to do homework after a short walk.

Kathy kept looking out the window to see if she was coming home. Finally, she saw Lisa running toward the house at top speed. As she got closer, she could see that her daughter was crying.

Kathy ran to open the door for her. "What's wrong, Lisa? Why are you upset?"

Almost incoherently, Lisa sputtered, "Mom, I stopped at Mathew's house to say I was sorry about what I'd said about you two getting married. He was really nice at first, saying it was okay and not to feel bad. He was sitting on the sofa, and he pulled me toward him. He grabbed me and sat me on his lap. He started to put his hands all over me. He kept wiggling, and I could feel a big lump under me. I was so scared that I started to cry. He put his hands up my dress, and I felt his hand touching me 'there.' When I screamed, I was able to push him away and get up. I ran out of his house and then home as fast as I could. Mom, do something. I told you lots of times he was always looking at me. I'm scared."

Kathy looked at her daughter. *She must be lying. She's trying to make Mathew out to be a monster. Oh God, what can I do? Is she telling the truth this time? Does she know what she is accusing Mathew of? I can't believe she's saying these things about Mathew.*

Lisa pushed her mother away. "You don't believe me, do you? You think he's a good person, don't you? I told you how he was—and you still won't believe me." She ran into the living room.

After a few minutes, Kathy heard Lisa talking on the phone. She didn't sound as hysterical as she had earlier. In fact, her voice was almost steady. *Who is she talking to? What is going on here?*

Lisa went upstairs and closed her door with a bang.

Kathy sat at the kitchen table in a daze. She finally got up and called Mathew. There was no answer. *Of course not—he's at work at this time of the day.* She dialed his work number, but it was busy. She waited a minute and dialed again. It was still busy.

Kathy went upstairs and tapped on Lisa's door. "Are you all right, Lisa? Can I come in? I need to hear your story again before I do anything about it."

"I already called Daddy, and he is on his way. I know he'll be able to do something about that man. He told me to call him anytime something was wrong."

*Lisa doesn't sound like she's still upset. If what she says is true, she would be still crying—not almost gleeful.*

Kathy went downstairs and stared out the window. Her mind was a chaotic jumble.

A police car and Bruce's car pulled into the driveway. *Bruce didn't wait long to call the police. Is he using Lisa to destroy Mathew—and me? He is a bitter man, but even he could not use his own daughter to get revenge. No he can't be that cruel.*

Kathy opened the door as the men walked up the driveway.

Bruce yelled, "Where is that son of a bitch? I'll kill him with my own hands if I get a hold of him."

"Now that's enough of that," the police officer said in a stern voice. "We don't have any proof of what you have told us." He turned to Kathy and said, "Mrs. Hilliard?"

Kathy nodded.

"My name is John Stephens, and I am from the sheriff's office. I am investigating an allegation that Mr. Kennedy improperly touched your daughter."

"Come in please, and you can tell me what's wrong," Kathy said quietly. She was trembling with shock. She turned and led them into the living room. "Please have a seat."

The officer sat on the sofa, and Bruce sat in a wing-back chair. The officer looked embarrassed as he drew out a notebook and began to read. He motioned to Bruce and said, "This man called me and said that your fiancé, Mathew Kennedy, improperly touched his daughter, Lisa. I will let him explain his call."

Bruce repeated Lisa's story.

Kathy listened carefully and then said, "Lisa is a child who makes up tales. She has had a problem with lying for a long time; in fact, it is so bad that I have made an appointment with a child psychiatrist. I believe that Mathew was at work today; he could not have done what Lisa claims." Kathy turned to Bruce. "We have not always seen things the same way, but you know that Lisa has a problem with lying. Do you think she is making this up so that you and I will get back together?"

Bruce sat up and thought about whether Lisa was so intent upon having the family together again that she'd make up a story like this. He was aware that Lisa lied, but it had never been like this. "Well, until I'm sure that he is proven innocent, I'll trust Lisa's word."

Officer Stephens asked, "May I speak to your daughter, Mrs. Hilliard?"

"Let me see if she is able to come down and talk to you."

Kathy went up to Lisa's room and knocked on the door. "Lisa, would you be able to talk to a police officer about what you've said happened at Mathew's house?"

When Lisa came out of her room, she looked ready to cry again. Kathy put her arms around her and tried to comfort her, but Lisa pushed her away.

Lisa said, "You don't believe me, do you?"

"No, I don't Lisa. I know Mathew well, and I don't believe he would do anything like that. Also, you have lied so many times that I just can't believe your story."

Lisa's eyes were filled with hate, and her face turned redder. She brushed past her mother and went down to the living room, but she stopped short of the room. The sight of the police officer and her father made her tremble.

Bruce jumped up and hugged her. "It's all right, little one. Just tell the officer what happened today in your own words. It will only take a few minutes. I'll be right here by you."

Kathy listened as Lisa told her tale through sobs and tears. She wondered what had happened to her lovely girl.

Lisa kept looking at her father for approval. When she finished, she said, "I have lied in the past, but this is what happened. It's the truth."

The police officer looked at Lisa and asked, "Are you telling the truth, Lisa? This is a serious charge. If you are lying about it and a jury believes you, Mr. Kennedy could go to prison."

Lisa looked at her father.

Bruce said, "My daughter would never lie about such a serious thing. That's right, isn't it? Lisa?"

She nodded.

"I need you to come back down to the station, Mr. Hilliard, to fill out some papers. We need to make this a legal charge so we can arrest Mr. Kennedy."

Kathy stood and said, "She is lying—and you know it. What kind of father are you to ask her to lie like this—just for revenge?" She turned to the officer and said, "I know my fiancé, and he did not do this. Lisa's father has been filling her head with lies about Mathew and me for months. How can I convince you that these charges are all lies?"

"Well," the officer replied, "the charges will have to be proven, of course, with a fair trial. The jury will want to make certain that he is guilty before passing judgment. I assure you that Mr. Kennedy will be shielded from any harm while waiting for his hearing and a trial."

The silence in the room made Kathy shiver. She felt like the world had stopped.

Lisa said, "Can I come and stay with you, Daddy? I don't feel good staying here when Mom doesn't believe me."

The police officer shook his head. "No, that change has to be made by the judge that heard the divorce case, not me. You father can ask and see if it can be changed."

Lisa turned and went upstairs.

Kathy turned to Bruce and said, "Just go now— and don't ever come here again. You will never be welcome at this house. You are a poor excuse for a man and a father."

Bruce said, "Kathy, try to understand. Lisa is my daughter too. I also want to be certain that she is telling the truth. A hearing and a trial is the only way I can be sure if he is innocent or guilty. I want to protect her from all harm. I wish I'd been more helpful with the girls, Kathy. I know Lisa lies, but I don't think she'd make up a story like this. I have to be sure. This is a horrible thing—if it really happened."

He looked haggard as he went out to his car. His steps were slow, like an old man, and his shoulders were slumped.

She watched the police car stop at Mathew's house. After a moment, it drove away. They would probably go to his workplace to arrest him. Kathy rubbed her forehead. It felt like it would explode. *What a nightmare this day has been. Can anything get worse?*

Kathy called Mathew's office and his home, but there was no word from him. She worried for the rest of the afternoon. When dinnertime came and there was still no word, she feared the worst. He would be in prison until there could be a hearing.

Dinner was quiet. Lisa ate and then went back to her room. Noreen was quiet and did not say anything about Mathew or her sister. After dinner, Noreen said she would do homework for a while.

Neither girl offered to help with dishes, but Kathy let them go. She was too drained to make waves.

# Chapter Nine

Kathy was up before dawn. Her head felt as if it had been hit with a hammer. Her first cup of coffee was welcome, and she nursed it as she thought about what to do. She decided to call Mathew's parents to see if they had any news. Since she was not Mathew's wife yet, she had no legal right to any information.

It took her a while to find their phone number because of her shaking hands. Her tears made everything blurry. She finally placed the call. It was early enough, she thought, that they would still be home. She tried to think of what to say. Would they even talk to her, knowing it was her daughter that put Mathew in prison?

A soft voice said, "Hello, this is Shirley Kennedy."

"This is Kathy Hilliard, Mrs. Kennedy. I know you must be outraged by what my daughter has done. I am calling you because I am at my wit's end. I haven't heard from Mathew, and I don't know how to get in touch with him. Can you help me?"

"Kathy, I am so worried that I can't think straight. I know he is innocent, and I can't figure why Lisa would say what she did. Is she psychotic?"

Kathy was dazed and upset; she didn't know what was going through her daughter's head. "I wish I knew what is happening to Lisa. She has always lied, but this is criminal. I am sorrier than I can say. My heart is breaking."

"We know that Mathew is innocent, and it will be proven. I can give you the phone number of Mathew's building, but I can't promise they will let you speak to him until after he sees his attorney. They say he is safe and won't be in danger there. I'll have his attorney call you, and he'll see what he can do. Okay?"

Kathy nodded and then realized Mathew's mother couldn't see her. "Thanks, Mrs. Kennedy."

"Please call me Shirley, Kathy. Mathew has told me how this trouble came about. I know this is not your fault. When we go to Burlington, we will try our best to meet with you. He is being detained until we can get bail. I don't know if he will be allowed bail yet. He will have a hearing in two weeks, and then there may be a trial, depending on the outcome of the hearing."

Kathy sighed. "Thank you for not blaming me for Lisa's lies. I should have taken steps to correct her lying before this. I never thought anything this horrible could happen. How is he holding up, Shirley? He must be out of his mind with worry and anger. I am sure you must be feeling the same way."

"We know he is innocent, and it will be proven in time. I trust in God to see that justice is done—and that your daughter gets the help she needs."

"Thank you for having faith in me. Is there is anything I can take to Mathew? How can I visit him? Where is he being held?"

"He is being held at a special prison to keep him safe. In a regular prison, he would not live long, even though he has not been proven guilty. The inmates would want to harm him. We can visit him, but I don't believe you can just now. We are getting a lawyer for him. There is nothing that he needs . . . except our prayers and our faith in him."

Kathy thanked her and disconnected. Almost numb with grief and fear, she let the tears flow.

<hr>

It was several days before Kathy could see Mathew. She was allowed to see him for a very short time, and a glass pane divided them. She hoped her smile was reassuring; her face felt like it was going to break with the effort. He tried to look confident, but his haggard face and the dark circles under his eyes told her how he really felt. His yellow coveralls gave his skin an odd, sickly hue.

He said, "Kathy, you are not to blame. Lisa is in trouble, and I hope we can get her to see what her lying has done. Also, you're her mom, and it must be heartbreaking to have to choose which of us to believe. If we can get Lisa the help she needs, she will tell the truth. If not, she will have many regrets when she is older and more mature."

The visit dragged. Kathy could not think of anything optimistic to say. She kept fiddling with her hair, trying to compose her thoughts. Her pink blouse and gray skirt didn't do anything to cheer him up. There was no way Kathy could change the situation.

She wished she could hug him to show how much she loved and trusted him.

---

The day before the hearing, Kathy had a bad feeling about it. If they found due cause, he would remain locked up until the trial. She tried to be optimistic, but the problems were too enormous.

At the hearing, several facts became clear. Mathew did not have an alibi for the whole afternoon of his alleged offense. He had been working alone; after lunch, he had made a delivery to a client's office. No one had been there, but he had been told to leave the computer at the front desk as he had done several times in the past. He left the computer with a note and had gone home—only to be arrested.

Bruce's attorney claimed he had gone home early and was there when Lisa came to visit. Mathew would have to face a trial, and he would remain in prison until then.

Kathy had to work the next day and heard the verdict at the hospital. The date for the trial was

April 28. She cried for an hour before finally getting herself under control.

Seeing Lisa every day was a mixed blessing. On one hand, she needed her to be home so she could take her to the psychiatrist's office. The first two sessions seemed to go well.

Bruce had asked if he could be at some of the sessions, and he had been invited to the next two.

He called every day to speak to Lisa, and she preened about like a movie queen.

Kathy found it hard to deal with Lisa, but she knew her daughter needed a stable life. Kathy kept her opinions unspoken and was as calm and loving as possible. After all, Lisa was only a child. Whatever underlying problems were causing her to lie could be brought to light and healed.

A recurring thought left a dark, hurtful, open wound. *Could Mathew be guilty? Could he have done what Lisa said he had? No! He was innocent. He was a kind caring man. No, Lisa was lying.* Torn between Mathew and Lisa, she prayed for a miracle.

# Chapter Ten

The trial was getting closer, and the media was searching for more details. The newspaper had publicized Lisa's history of lying—but had withheld her name. Lisa had been warned to keep quiet at school. So far, she had not been publicly involved.

Lisa was seeing Dr. Silverman regularly, but her story had not changed. Dr. Silverman's visits with Lisa and her father had brought to light one underlying problem. Lisa was obsessed with gaining her father's approval and love. Dr. Silverman had made the connection and hoped to help Lisa understand her feelings. If her father could understand Lisa's needs, there could be healing.

Bruce was surprised to realize that Lisa thought he was not proud of her and didn't love her.

Dr. Silverman asked Bruce to remember any occasion when he had been uncaring or thoughtless with Lisa.

He had been busy and sometimes distracted, but he had never hurt her feelings. He admitted to speaking badly about Kathy. He wanted her back—but not at the expense of his daughter's emotional health. He claimed he was unaware of upsetting the girls with his criticisms of Kathy. He tried to hide his shame, but his red face gave him away.

Dr. Silverman nodded and asked if he had forgotten an incident or two. "Please give this some more thought, Bruce. If you remember an incident when Lisa could have thought you didn't love her, let me know."

Weeks later, he made a private appointment with Dr. Silverman to ask what he could do to help Lisa. He thought about the times the girls had been with him. Had he criticized Kathy too much? Was he to blame? What if Lisa had lied to make Mathew look like a bad person so her mother and he could reunite? The thought brought chills to his skin and a nightmare of a headache. *No, that can't be. She's just a child. Sure I told her how her mother had made me feel, but I never meant to cause this trouble. I resent Mathew, but I don't want him in prison.*

At home, Lisa kept to her room. She did her homework but showed no enthusiasm for drawing or painting. She never rode the bike Mathew had given her. She was worried that the jury would say she lied—and everyone would know it. If they found out, no one would speak to her again. She'd never have any friends. Telling stories had been fun, but if they stopped believing her, she'd be laughed at and gossiped about for a long time—maybe forever. She stormed around the room, knocking things over and feeling as if she'd burst.

Night after night, Lisa dreamed of people pointing at her and saying, "Liar, liar." She couldn't keep her mind on her studies, and the dark circles under her eyes and her puffy skin told a tale of strain and distress.

---

The trial began with intense testimony. Lisa's story was told—with emphasis on her having told her mother about prior spying incidents. Lisa's lying was an important factor, and Mathew's attorney thought that it—and Mathew's good character—made the charges look false. Mathew's family began to hope for an acquittal as Lisa's many lies were recounted.

The last day of the trial went well for Mathew. Most of the news had stressed that the girl was a habitual liar whose word could not be relied upon. Mathew had strong moral values and no previous record. Almost everything pointed toward an acquittal.

---

Lisa crept into Noreen's bedroom when she knew her mom was asleep. She gently whispered her sister's name. When she had Noreen's attention, she started to cry. Between sobs, she said, "He is going to go free, and everyone will call me a liar. Everyone will talk me about. Somehow they will find my name and point at me. I can't stand it! I won't ever be happy again. Will you help me, Noreen?

"I know I have been mean to you in the past, but I swear I will never be mean again if you will do what I ask. We are sisters, and I love you. I'd do the same for you if you asked me."

"What? What are you asking me to do, Lisa?"

"I need you to say that Mathew has touched you too, but you were too scared to tell. If you tell Mom that—and cry a little—she'll believe you. You have never lied to her before."

Noreen gasped and sat up. She was as stiff as a board. "I have done many things for you, but telling that kind of lie is—no, no, I can't do it! You are being mean to even ask me. I can't hurt Mathew for you and lie to Mom . . . never."

Lisa was crying louder, and Noreen was afraid her mother would wake up. "Shush, Lisa. You did this for some silly reason . . . and now you want me to help them put Mathew in prison for a long time. I like him. I really do. I can't help you on this, Lisa. If I were you, I'd tell Mom what you did and then Mathew would go free."

"Oh, Noreen. I can't do that. Can't you see that if people know I lied, they would say I was a liar forever? Mom would hate me, and Dad would never love me. Please help me. Please do this one thing for me. I will never be mean or ask you for anything . . . ever."

Noreen thought about what Lisa had said. *If I do this, Lisa will be happy again. Mathew is a really nice man, and the jury will never say he did this.*

Noreen said, "Lisa, I think I can help you, but you have to promise me something and really, really mean it."

"I will do anything, Noreen. Just tell me what I have to do."

"Never, ever lie again."

"I promise you, Lisa, that I will never tell a lie again . . . no matter what."

"That's a promise you have to keep. If you break it, I will tell everyone that you lied about Mathew."

Lisa nodded and hugged her sister. Relieved and hoping that her problems would soon end, Lisa crept back to her bed.

Noreen tried to sleep, but the sun was up. She regretted her promise and wanted to take it back. Somehow she had to lie to her mother—something she had never done before.

❧

Noreen waited until she was home from school the next day to tell her big lie. She felt queasy and had to bite her lips several times before beginning. "Mom, I have been keeping quiet about something important because I did not want to upset you."

"Tell me, Noreen. I am listening."

She did not have to make up the tears; she hurt so badly that she cried and sobbed. Her body shook and jerked. "I did not want Mathew to go to jail because I liked him, but he did the same thing to me as he did to Lisa."

"What! What are you saying, Noreen? I don't believe this. You kept this back so I wouldn't feel upset? Good God, child, are you really sure of what you are saying?"

Noreen nodded, unable to speak.

Kathy patted her and rocked her like a baby. "Noreen, you were wrong not to tell us what happened. I have to call Mathew's attorney. It will change everything. The trial will be all but over. Mathew will go to prison. Oh my God! Help me— and forgive Mathew. Don't say anything to anyone about this, Noreen. I have to go make that call now."

Noreen watched her mom drag herself to the phone. *Why did I ever promise to lie for Lisa? I wish I could take it all back.*

Noreen met Lisa by the lake to tell her that she had lied for her. Both girls felt miserable, but they vowed to remain silent.

Lisa was relieved that no one would know her secret. She was safe.

When Kathy called Mathew's attorney, the words would not come at first. She was hysterical. Kathy finally explained what Noreen had told her, and he felt as if he had been hit in his gut. He couldn't speak. His mind seemed to have crashed. Silently he replaced the receiver. He knew the trial was over as far as Mathew was concerned.

Later, when he was calmer, he dialed Kathy's number. Over and over he had Kathy tell him exactly what Noreen had said. It was unbelievable. Something was very wrong here. He felt it, knew it was there, but could not think of how to reveal it. He felt certain that Mathew was innocent. Now he would go to prison based on lies told by two young girls.

The rest of the day was a blur to Kathy. She thought about Mathew, the trial, and his kindness to her and the girls. *He must have done it if Noreen said so. She never lies. Oh, to know the truth. I can believe Mathew because I love him and have faith in him or I can despise him for doing this to my girls.*

------

The courtroom was filled to capacity the next morning. TV cameras were already in position, and reporters were eager to make the headline for the day. The hush was broken when the attorney for Mr. Hilliard began to present his new evidence. Loud mummers broke out, and the judge hammered for quiet.

Both sides made their last statements, and the jury went to deliberate.

The verdict—guilty as charged—brought cries of unbelief.

People shouted, "What an upset! Is that nice young man really guilty?"

The sentencing would be decided in a few days. The judge banged his gavel to signify the end of the trial.

When the room cleared, Mathew's attorney remained in his seat. He knew justice had not been served, but he was unable to prove it.

# Chapter Eleven

Kathy did not attend the trial. She awoke feeling numb and half sick. She could not keep down her morning coffee, and she barely made it to the bathroom. She jumped at every sound. The girls were at school, and she had called in sick. She knew she couldn't cope if she had gone to the trial. She'd be lucky to have a job if this kept up.

She had to pull herself together. There were many tomorrows to face, and she would need courage and more. Perhaps prayer would help? She meditated for a few minutes. She asked for peace for Mathew—and both families. When she rose, she felt calmer and had the strength to face whatever the day brought.

She turned the TV to the local channel. The trial would not take long after Noreen's confession. She busied herself with watering plants, planning for dinner, and straightening the rooms. When she heard a roar from the TV, she hurried to see what it was about. When the trial was over, the verdict was guilty as charged.

She watched Mathew with his head bowed. When he looked up, his face wore a stunned look. His shoulders sagged, and he closed his eyes in pain. *Well, he deserves to be in pain, doesn't he? He isn't the man I thought he was. How could he do this to my daughters? How could he frighten a child, one he knew well and said he cared for?*

Kathy looked again, but the camera was on the judge and to the jury as they filed out. The camera zoomed back to Mathew. He was scanning the room as if he was looking for someone. Then he slumped forward in his chair and stared at the floor.

For the first time in days, Kathy searched her soul. Was he really guilty or had the girls made up a lie? She was soon lost in memories of her time with Mathew. When had he shown signs of being a corrupt person? The answer was never. She recalled the many times he had come in for coffee. They had talked about so many things. They shared their love of books and plays—and a dislike of hard rock music. They also spoke of childhood, dreams for the future, and plans for travel with the girls.

He had always been attentive to her views. When they had become lovers, he was tender, passionate, and caring. He liked to watch nature and was interested in gardening. His herb garden was full of special spices and herbs, and he had given her a jar of dried mint for her tea.

All of this gave her a jolt of awareness. He wasn't the kind of person to do such a terrible thing. She didn't want to believe that her daughters were lying, but she didn't believe he was guilty. How would she ever know the truth? He was going to prison, and people would believe he was guilty. How would he be treated in prison? Were the stories true about other inmates killing child molesters?

She would take Noreen to Dr. Silverman for sessions. Both girls would need special care now. She could only hope that, if the girls were lying, they would confess soon. In the meantime, she had to walk carefully and not give in to her doubts about Mathew's guilt. Deep in her heart, she believed him to be innocent, but terrible thoughts bombarded her.

She went to the door and saw Skipper. He was looking out at the road, waiting for Mathew. She had tied him to a post for an hour, and now she should take him for a walk. After fastening a lead on Skipper and Sheeba, she walked toward the lake. It was a cool day, but the fresh air made her feel a lot better. She decided to have faith in Mathew regardless of what her daughters said. She came home with renewed energy. Love included faith, trust, and caring; she had all these and more for Mathew.

She wrote him a long, loving letter. She poured out her thoughts and her love. She promised to keep taking the girls to Dr. Silverman in the hopes that they would confess their lies. She tried to be cheerful and keep his hopes alive, even when she knew it was almost a lost cause. She wrote about Skipper and their walks and how the two dogs were inseparable. She enclosed a picture of the dogs sitting up begging. Her love for him was clear on every page.

———◆———

Mathew was slumped in a chair at his prison cell. *What a goddamn day this has been.* The brutal punch to his gut was Noreen's lie. She had seemed to be the one person who was truthful. What had made her do this? Lisa and her need to protect her lie was probably it. She must have known that the trial was near the end and just needed Noreen to back her up. He hoped that Dr. Silverman could help unravel the cause of Lisa's lies. Lisa was just a child, and he was certain that she didn't know the enormity of her lie or the consequences.

He had been given a sentence of one year, but he could well be dead in a few days or weeks. Instead of being in a correctional institute, he was in a prison for serious offenders. There was no room at the correctional prison for a week or two. He hoped to God they knew he was only in there for a short while. An unwritten rule was to remove any convicted child molester. He shivered. What if they thought he had hurt the girl? He was not ready to die yet. What could he do to escape revenge if they thought he was guilty? He mulled this over until he came up with an idea.

At dinnertime, he asked a guard who the prison chaplain was.

"Hey, do you know him? Could you ask if I could meet him soon?"

"Nuthin' doin'. I'm not your errand boy."

"No offense meant, buddy. I'm new here. How about some cigarettes? I have a pack in my cell."

"Okay, give me them at dinner. I'll tell the reverend you want to see him, but it might take several days."

Mathew nodded. If he pushed it, he might never see Reverend Tierney. "Thanks for doing that for me," he said quietly.

A few days later the chaplain came to see Mathew. When he heard Mathew's request, he raised his eyebrows in surprise. No one had ever asked him that before. He listened to Mathew's story.

Mathew asked for three weeks of grace. Could the inmates give him that time?

Reverend Tierney studied Mathew for a moment and said, "Yes. I will be pleased to do that. I hope it works for you."

Reverend Tierney asked for a meeting with the inmates of the whole section that included Mathew's cell. When he had their attention, he asked for their consideration and explained Mathew's situation. He didn't mention anything about what had been done to child molesters in the past. He asked them to give Mathew four weeks before passing judgment. He added that their best behavior would be in their best interests.

There was silence after the chaplain spoke.

Each man tried to decide what to do. No one had ever asked for a time limit before. The idea was nuts, but what could be the harm in waiting? He wasn't going anywhere.

The chaplain had been fair to them over the years. He had made the holidays less stressful and brought special treats to them.

The leader said, "We will talk this over and let you know in a week. If the child can be brought to recant her lie, then okay. If not, she must be telling the truth."

———◆◆◆———

Buffer's cell was next to Pulaski's cell. They had been friends for a long time.

"Hey, Pulaski, what do you think of the request? I hear that guy had someone that was close to him on the jury. That's why he only got a year. Christ, it pays to have friends in high places."

"Where did you hear that, Buffer? I ain't heard nothing like that. Do ya think he's for real?"

"I can't tell, but he must be running scared to go the reverend for help. I don't believe him one bit. He's tryin' to pull a fast one, that's all."

"Ya gonna vote no? If you do, I will too. We don't owe him a freakin' thing, and I'm ready for a little fun."

When the men met again, they grumbled their replies. Reverend Tierney knew it would be a miracle if they agreed to Mathew's request. The answer was partly an "okay," but some men did not agree. It was not a real stay for Mathew after all. He'd have to watch his back. The chaplain thanked them and left to do his rounds for the day. He knew better than to pressure them.

About a week later, the chaplain nodded to Mathew. It had been unorthodox for him to speak to the inmates, but he had taken a chance. Even though it was not unanimous, he hoped it would help Mathew to at least gain time.

Mathew shrugged and said, "I'll have to watch my back, but I appreciate your trying."

Mathew hoped the inmates would all give him time. Maybe he'd get lucky and be sent to another facility soon. He was counting on Kathy and Dr. Silverman—and praying against all odds that Lisa would see what evil her lie had done and admit it.

In the meantime, he would watch Buffer and Pulaski every minute they were near him.

# *Chapter Twelve*

Dr. Silverman greeted Lisa, Noreen, and Kathy. They sat in comfortable chairs and chatted about school for a few minutes.

Dr. Silverman noted Lisa's pale face and Noreen's listless manner. She nodded at Lisa and said, "You don't look as if you are feeling well, Lisa. Are you all right?"

Lisa replied, "Yes, I'm fine. School is just getting harder now. We have lots of tests."

"I see. And you, Noreen? Do you feel all right too?"

Noreen nodded.

They discussed their last visit with their dad, Lisa's painting, and friends at school. When asked, both girls said they were glad the trial was over. They showed no signs of tension or nervousness, but they kept looking at each other.

Dr. Silverman was certain they were hiding something, but she didn't want to use shock to find out. She had to help them accept what had happened and get back to a normal life. The other was to discover the truth, if possible. Kathy had said that there were no nightmares or sudden bursts of tears, but the girls could be keeping these things from her.

After they talked about Skipper, it was time to go. Dr. Silverman not discovered the reason behind their lies. There was a reason—she was sure of it. Getting them to open up was the problem.

"I'd like to see you alone next week, Lisa. The following one, I'd like to see you alone, Noreen. Have some fun after school and get outdoors more if you can. You both look pale and wan to me." She turned to Kathy and said, "Are they eating well, Mrs. Hilliard?"

"Not like they usually do, but we've had some rainy days, and school has been more taxing."

---

Time seemed to go slower than ever, but Mathew tried to keep his mind from thoughts that would make him mad. Thinking of Kathy and the many hours they had shared soothed his spirits. He recalled their closeness and her sweet giving as they each found the joy of passion and deep caring. He relived each moment of touching her and her cries of release. They had delighted in finding ways to please each other.

The memories brought joy—and some pain. His future held lonely days and nights filled with fear. What the inmates would do became a daily obsession.

Buffer had said, "There's a time to come when you won't be here, buddy."

Pulaski had said, "Your neck feelin' okay? We're on to you. Don't forget it."

Sometimes it was just a gesture, a raised fist, or a slicing movement across Buffer's neck, but it was more deadly than words.

He kept hoping for a move to the correctional institute, but after two weeks, he was still waiting for the promised move. Only the thought of Kathy's belief in him gave him any peace and hope. At night, alone in his cell, fear stalked him for hours until he fell asleep.

The days crept by, and Mathew grew more despondent. He thought of Kathy and the year ahead. She would be alone. He wondered if it would be better for her if he confessed. She would be enraged at first, but she might find someone who would be a loving companion. He was a goner if Lisa did not confess within two weeks. The thought did not please him, but it was a way for Kathy to find happiness later on. He loved her more than he loved his own life.

The thought of Lisa knowing he confessed when he was innocent made him stop and rethink his plan. She would spend the rest of her life knowing her lies were the reason he died. No child should have that on his or her conscience. But if he remained silent, she would still be devastated when he died. He had no control over that. He closed his eyes, and the waves of despair came again and robbed him of his ability to concentrate.

He would not confess to doing something he was not capable of. He prayed again for a way out and deliverance from what was to come. He prayed for Lisa and Noreen. *How can I let them know that I forgive them? They are just children, troubled ones at that. I don't think they know how much damage they have done. They will later on though, but it will be too late to make a difference.*

He closed his eyes and concentrated on Lisa and Noreen. *Tell the truth. Tell the truth. Tell the truth.* It was his mantra for days. He repeated it with a prayer in his heart.

---

When Lisa came into Dr. Silverman's office, she knew what the lady was going to try to do. She would keep quiet and then go home. Her secret would be safe. She sat and waited for the questions.

Dr. Silverman smiled and said, "I hear you love to paint, Lisa. Have you had lessons? What do you use for a medium? Watercolors? Oil?"

"I like to sketch first, and then I decide what to use—oil, colored pencils, or crayons. Watercolor is hard to do if you've had no lessons."

"I'd like to see one of your paintings, Lisa. Would you bring one in for me to see the next time you come?"

"Okay, Dr. Silverman, but you may not like it. My father didn't like the one I did for him, although I thought it was my best."

*Thank God, an opening at last.* Dr. Silverman smiled and said, "Perhaps he was too busy to really look. I think dads are sometimes so tired they don't pay attention."

"No. He told me it was okay, but I needed more lessons."

"I bet that hurt your feelings, Lisa. Has he ever said anything more about your artwork?"

"No, I didn't show him anymore. Besides, I know we can't afford lessons. My art teacher at school says I am good at drawing and making things look real. So I keep practicing at home."

"Good for you, Lisa. Do you think your dad would have more time to look at your artwork if you lived with him?"

Lisa nodded. "Well, of course. If we lived together again, he would have more time for me. He wants to have Mom go back to him . . . and so do I."

"Don't you think that's up to your mom to decide that? She was not happy before. Perhaps it's better to live apart than to argue all the time."

Lisa scowled and shifted in her chair.

After more talk of art, Dr. Silverman said, "I think we have done enough for today. I will see Noreen next week and then both of you the following one. I hope you have a good week. School will be over on Friday, and I hope you have plans for a summer of fun. Keep on enjoying your art. Your mom tells me you are gifted."

Lisa smiled and said good-bye, happy not to have revealed her secret.

Dr. Silverman felt she had been given a look into what was bothering Lisa. Now, how could she use it to help Lisa and Noreen? Buried inside this young girl was the reason for her turmoil. It had to be more serious than her father not liking her drawing. Rejection could be hard for a child, and Lisa may have thought her father did not want her or love her. If she could be certain of it, many lives could be changed—and perhaps a man's life could be saved.

She called Mrs. Hilliard and told her about what Lisa had revealed. "It is just a small insight, Mrs. Hilliard. Do you recall Lisa ever mentioning this to you?"

Kathy thought for a moment and said, "No, not really. Several months ago, Lisa came home and was very quiet. That may have been the time her father rejected her gift. But it is not the first time. When we all were together as a family, he didn't pay much attention to either girl. His work and my life outside of the home were uppermost in his mind. I went to school functions and took them to piano lessons and games. Lisa remembers only what she thinks is real. She blocks out what doesn't fit her memories."

"That is part of an obsession. Once the idea is fixed in the mind, every incident seems to reinforce it. I have a feeling we are on the right path. I will talk to you again after seeing Noreen. Bye."

# Chapter Thirteen

Kathy was trying to keep her caring, loving attitude toward the girls. At home, she never mentioned Mathew. She wrote to him every day and poured out her love for him. She kept him up to date on the visits to Dr. Silverman, and even though they showed no positive results, she tried to be upbeat and encouraging.

The girls seemed, by mutual consent, to avoid being with her. They did homework in their rooms or went for long walks to the lake.

They all tried to avoid speaking of Mathew, although his name was in their thoughts.

The days went faster as June approached. School was winding down, and there were final tests and outings.

Lisa's class had a barbeque at Red Rocks Park, a popular spot by the lake for picnics. Lisa hoped to sketch the mountains on the New York side of Lake Champlain. The day was clear and warm. The wind was pleasantly soft off the lake. Lisa was told to clean up around her desk, and she was the last to leave her room for the bus. As she walked toward the exit, she overheard two teachers talking about a man who had been convicted of child molestation.

*Child molestation? What does that mean?* She listened more closely and realized they were speaking of Mathew. Her heart nearly stopped when her gym teacher said, "I give him another week at most. Then he will be wiped out by the inmates there."

*Wiped out? Do they mean kill him? They couldn't mean that, could they?*

Lisa hardly knew what she was doing. She got on the bus, but she didn't see any of the passing trees or buildings. She sat in shock, telling herself it was not true. It couldn't be true. He was only going to prison for a little while, maybe a year or so. But then he would go free, wouldn't he?

When Lisa arrived at the picnic spot, she asked if she could sit by the pine trees and look out at the Adirondack Mountains. She went to a large rock and sat against it. The view was breathtaking; each peak was etched dark against the sky. Her thoughts cleared as she focused on what she had heard.

*What made me tell such a lie? What made me think that being back with Dad would make me happy? I've not been happy since the day I lied about Mathew. Now I am the cause of his being in prison, and everyone is hurting because of me.* Tears rolled down her face, and a sob broke free from her soul. She wiped her eyes and looked around to see if anyone had seen her crying.

She saw a large brown dog sitting among the pine needles with his head resting on his front paws. He was looking straight at her. She thought she could feel his eyes speaking to her. She turned back to the mountains and felt uneasy, but she knew the dog would not hurt her.

She remembered how kind Mathew had been to her. More tears ran down her face as she thought of Christmas and the beautiful red bike. She recalled the many ski trips they had shared, and Mathew always seeing that she had a good lunch. He had teased about her love of desserts, but he always saw that she had one.

The dog moved closer to her. She carefully reached out and patted his head. He sat beside her and looked out across the lake. She wondered if he was lost. He wore a collar, and his fur was brushed and clean. His eyes focused on hers. They were brown like Mathew's eyes, and his gentle look spoke to her. It was almost as if Mathew was sending her a message. In a weird way, she felt it was true.

*What message would Mathew send me anyway? Perhaps "I hate you, Lisa," or "You are a terrible child, Lisa." But no, the eyes were warm and forgiving. If he is sending a message, it is of love and forgiveness—not hate. It was as if he was saying, "Tell the truth, Lisa. Please tell the truth."*

*Oh God, I wish I could make it all right again. How can I do that? What can I do now that I've lied? Mathew is locked in prison. He might even be killed because of me. If I tell, everyone will know I lied. They will know what a terrible person I am. I won't ever have friends again. And Dad will turn his back on me forever. No one will love me if I confess.*

Lisa realized that she had no friends, and her dad had never shared his time when they lived together. Her mom and dad would never get together again. Nothing had gone right since she had lied. She was the only one who knew the truth about her lie, but she could set things right again.

The dog put his paw on her shoulder and softly woofed. He soon disappeared into the pines.

Lisa again looked out at the mountains. She would like to paint them someday. Looking back one more time, she went to the teacher in charge and asked to be taken home. She claimed her stomach hurt; for once, it was not a lie.

---

Her mother wasn't home from work when Lisa came home. She waited and prayed until she heard her mother's car come into the driveway.

Kathy asked, "What is it, Lisa? Are you all right? How come you are home so early?"

Lisa stood and tried to stop trembling. She had to tell her mother what she had done. She took a shaky breath, and said, "Mom, I have to tell you something. I hope you will listen and not hate me."

Kathy reached out to hug Lisa. "I would never hate you—no matter what you did. Just tell me what's wrong. I will listen—with my ears and my heart."

The whole story poured out between sobs and hiccups. "Mom, I overheard some girls talking about a man who had touched a little girl and had to go to prison for it. I thought that if I said Mathew had done that to me, he would go away forever. Then our family could get together again."

Kathy rocked Lisa like a baby, trying to sooth her daughter's anguish. When she spoke, it was with a voice so low that Lisa could hardly hear her. "Lisa, I know you did the wrong thing, but you are still a child. In some ways, you are naive and unaware of the enormity of what happened. Yes, I think Mathew will forgive you. He has worried about you ever since this happened." Suddenly a feeling of urgency drove her to say, "Lisa, I have to make a phone call, and it's to save Mathew from harm. I will only be a minute."

She ran to the phone and tried to find the number she needed. Her thoughts were so scrambled that she couldn't think of where to look. She dialed 411 and asked for the number. It rang and rang as Kathy hopped from one foot to the other.

At last she heard a voice. It was a secretary who said she was very busy, but if she would leave a message, someone would get back to her soon.

Kathy said it was an emergency and had to speak with the district attorney. She quickly explained why and was suddenly connected to him. She told him that her daughter had just confessed to lying about the incident.

"How did this confession come about? What happened to make her confess?" he asked.

"Please. I am so worried that he will be harmed in prison. I had to call you as soon as I heard what my daughter said. Can you protect him until you can verify what I have told you?"

"Yes, I will personally make the call. You are aware that we will have to speak with your daughter to bring this to the correct conclusion. Will she cooperate with us?"

Kathy crossed her fingers. "Yes, as of right now, Lisa wants to tell what she has done. She admits to the lie and coercing her sister."

"I promise to see that Mathew is removed from his current prison immediately and sent to a safer one. I hope this is going to be resolved soon. I felt all along that there was a flaw in your daughter's story; it just couldn't be proven."

Kathy went back to Lisa and told her that Mathew would be safe. She assured Lisa that she was forgiven and that Mathew would forgive her too. She hugged Lisa close and said, "I love you. Don't ever forget that."

Kathy fixed lunch since Lisa had missed it, and then they shared a cup of tea and cookies. When Noreen came home from school, they told her the news.

"Oh, I am so happy that you told the truth, Lisa. Now I can be happy and feel good about myself again."

"The people who talk will not do that for long. Soon they will forget, and you'll make new friends."

Kathy was not so sure of that, and an idea formed in her mind that could help Lisa over the rough spots. If everyone agreed, it could be the answer.

---

Later that evening when the girls were upstairs talking and comparing some summer plans, Kathy called Dr. Silverman. She explained all that had happened and her idea of Lisa living with her father for a while. Her idea was met with approval and Kathy called Bruce.

"Bruce, I have had quite a day. Lisa confessed to lying about Mathew and getting Noreen to lie as well. I've called the district attorney, and they are moving Mathew to a safer prison until he can be legally freed. I think it would be good if Lisa came to live with you, at least for a few months. When this has all calmed down, she could come home again. She wants to be with you, and it's okay with me. I think it would be best for her. It will protect her from any gossip that may be hurtful."

"I am sorry, Kathy, that I did not take more time with my girls. You have done a good job, and a lot of Lisa's problems are my fault. I let my jealousy and anger take control. I often spoke badly about you.

Lisa must have taken it all seriously. I am sorry I was not a better husband and father. I would like to have Lisa live with me, and both girls can come for special times. I can afford to give Lisa art lessons and will bite my tongue before saying anything negative."

Kathy almost laughed at that remark. Bruce would have to relearn patience and a good attitude fast if he was to help Lisa.

The next call was to Mathew's parents. She had tried to reach them several times, but they couldn't connect. She left an urgent message for them to call her. When she finally was able to speak with them, they were almost speechless with delight and relief. Kathy explained that it would take days before the release could be made official, but she thought it would be five days at the most.

She called her parents and gave them the news. They were guarded when told about Lisa living with her father, but they agreed that it would be best—at least for a little while.

Kathy couldn't sleep. She tossed and turned for hours, and she finally gave up. She tiptoed downstairs, sat in the cozy rocker, and cuddled Skipper. "Oh, sweetie, we can all go walking again. Mathew and I can look at the sunsets together and cuddle in bed at the end of the day."

The thought of what else they could do in bed made her squirm with anticipation.

Lisa felt relief that she could go to her father's house to live. She would not have to be the butt of the gossip that was certain to follow her. Her lies had made her a target of spiteful remarks. The lies seemed to get bigger with each telling.

Lisa worried every day about Mathew and what would happen when they met again. She had been reassured that he loved her and forgave her, but it did not seem real to her. She busied herself with her painting and helping with chores. She stayed alone most of the time.

She took extra pains with Skipper. Each day, she took both dogs for walks along the lake path. She talked to Skipper about what she had done, but his brown eyes did not send a message. She thought about the big brown dog and wondered what had become of him. She would never forget his loving eyes and what he seemed to be telling her: *Tell the truth. Tell the truth.*

---

For Mathew, the days of waiting were almost unbearable. He knew everyone was doing their best to speed the process up, but it was too slow for him. He counted the minutes and tried to keep a level head. *How long will it take? What could be the delay? Has something happened to drag out the process?*

At last, they told him that he would be a free man again in a few days. He tried to see himself as

Kathy would. Had he grown harder in prison? Did the shave really look okay? The water had been lukewarm, and the razor was old. His suit still fit, but it was a lot looser. Did she still love him? Had her feelings changed? He wished he had the answers. The questions came in rapid succession, taking him in circles.

Was Kathy upset because Lisa was going to live with Bruce? Would Noreen miss her sister and want to go there as well? How could he help them with all the problems his coming home would bring? Did he still have a job? No one had come to see him or get in touch with him since his arrest. It was not a big worry; he hoped to have an office of his own and be independent. He knew he could do it with Kathy's encouragement. His thoughts went around and around, but there were no answers. *I hope all goes well. After all these months, I can't wait for freedom—and to see and hold them again.*

---

Kathy put on her best spring dress. She didn't have a new one to wear, but she knew Mathew wouldn't notice. She checked her makeup, her hair, and her nylons. All seemed to be the best she could do. At the last moment, an idea brought a smile to her face. She ran back into the house.

Mathew saw the sun shining, and the sky was so blue it hurt his eyes. He paced until the gate opened.

He started walking down the gravel path to the car park. In the distance, beyond the barrier, he could see his mother and father. He also saw Kathy and the girls looking toward him with smiles of welcome. Kathy's mom and dad were waiting with open arms.

A blur of fur raced up the path to him. Skipper leaped into his arms, and he got a wet face from all the love in Skipper's heart.

In a few minutes, he was busy hugging and kissing all of them. He thought he would die of joy, if it were possible. He couldn't speak. He just rocked each one in a warm embrace. The circle was complete at last. No love could be greater than that of his family and Kathy. They had loved and trusted him through it all.

When they arrived at Kathy's house, she invited them in for lunch. Kathy had made three quiches with spinach and ham. She also had pitchers of iced tea and some sodas. There were four kinds of cookies for dessert; Kathy grinned when she saw how Mathew enjoyed them.

Mathew asked if Lisa would let him speak with her. She nodded, and they went into the living room. They sat on the sofa.

"Lisa, I know that when you told your lie to your mother, you did not know what the consequences would be. You could not know. I want you to know that I forgive you, and I hope you can put this all aside and not let it be a bad time for you. I am glad to be home and also happy that you will be able to live with your dad since that is what you want. You can come home anytime you wish. You will have two homes instead of one. Let's have a hug here. No more thoughts of the past, okay?

One more thing, Lisa. When I say I forgive you, I also want you to forgive yourself. Then just let it go. Don't keep bringing it back again and again. Real forgiveness includes putting it all behind you. You have found out why you lied. That is good. Now you can be a happy girl again. That's what I want more than anything."

He gave her a hug and saw a happy smile in return. He was relieved that all had gone smoothly. Lisa had such potential that it would be a crime if she couldn't be able to achieve her best.

"Mathew?"

"What, Lisa?"

"I have made a promise to never lie again."

"That's a good promise, Lisa. I know it will be one you keep."

They all had coffee or iced tea and sat in comfortable silence.

Lisa looked at Mathew and said, "Mathew, did I tell you about seeing a really huge brown dog at the park? It was humongous and had big golden-brown eyes. When I looked into his eyes, you won't believe what happened!"

Mathew groaned. *Not another whopper! Well, she did promise. She may be telling the truth. I'll give her a chance this time.*

"Go ahead, Lisa. I'm listening."

# About No Greater Love

After Kathy's divorce, she worked hard at being a good mother. Her two daughters spent every other weekend with their father, Bruce. After each visit with their father, Lisa, thirteen years old, was sullen and unhappy. Kathy knew Bruce told the girls lies about her. Lisa wanted her mom and dad to get back together again since she craved his attention and love.

Kathy meets a neighbor, and she is attracted to Mathew. Their romance blossoms, and they plan a wedding. Lisa wants to stop their plans and tells a vicious lie about Mathew.

Kathy believes him innocent since Lisa has been a compulsive liar for a long time, and she knows Mathew could not have done something so terrible. After a hearing, Mathew's trial begins. Due to Lisa's history of lying, most people do not believe her. She coerces her sister Noreen into lying for her and accuses Mathew of improper acts that frightened her. The jury found him guilty, and he is sentenced to a year in prison.

Once there, he knows his life is going to be short—his cellmates find a way of getting rid of child molesters. What can he and Kathy do? Can Lisa be made to see what she has done and tell the truth in time? They need a miracle—perhaps the miracle of love?